WHAT READERS ARE SAYING . . .

"As much as I wanted Wood's Colbie Colleen Series to continue, I was thrilled when the author introduced a new character and a new series! Didn't disappoint!" —B. Minch

"If you want to read a great mystery, don't miss one of Wood's books! Her new detective is great!" —Kasey Brandeis

"For me, a great book is one I can read in a day or two, then put it away, satisfied I spent my time well—Where Truth Goes to Die hooked me from the first page!" —Mary. C.

"Wood's books always tackle something I can relate to, and Where Truth Goes to Die made me think from the first chapter. Don't miss this book!" —Pauline

"Normally, I don't like to read—but, when someone introduced me to Wood's books a few years ago, I couldn't wait for her new one to come out! I haven't missed one!" —K.W.

"Great book! Then again, I'm not surprised—thanks for the fun read!" —M. Katz

"Give me more!" —Ronnie S.

Where Truth Goes to Die

A DECKLIN KILGARRY SUSPENSE MYSTERY—BOOK 1

Where Truth Goes to Die

A DECKLIN KILGARRY SUSPENSE MYSTERY—BOOK 1

Faith Wood

Faith Wood (signature)

WOOD MEDIA
BRITISH COLUMBIA, CANADA

Copyright © 2021 Faith Wood
Where Truth Goes to Die
A Decklin Kilgarry Suspense Mystery—Book 1
First Edition, Paperback 2021

All rights reserved. You may not use or reproduce by any means including graphic, electronic, or mechanical, photocopying, recording, taping, or by any information storage retrieval system without the written permission of the publisher. The only exception is using brief quotations embodied in critical articles or reviews.

ISBN: 979-8-88525-697-1

Printed in the United States of America

DEDICATION

I'm excited to introduce you to my new series!
Meet Decklin Kilgarry . . .

Chapter 1

No one enjoys an abrupt and unanticipated about-face when it comes to life—so, when things got sticky for Decklin Kilgarry, it was a time he didn't particularly enjoy. A duality he didn't quite understand. Then again, from his perspective, annihilate his trust, and it was goodnight Irene. Over. No tearful goodbyes.

A black and white thing.

No one suspected—or, if they did, no one said a word, leaving Kilgarry with the suspicion he was the only one. But, knowing his wife, there was probably more than one neighbor who peered out their picture window, wondering what was going on next door or across the street.

So—after a year of his wife's purposeful infidelity—when it became clear duplicity was going to be part of his daily existence, in his mind, there was no solution but to call it quits. No longer was he interested in making things work or waiting until the kids were out of school to leave his wife standing on the doorstep, blubbering.

Stooping to kiss their German shepherd on his head, he closed the front door without saying a word, no longer standing at the crossroads. No longer shackled.

No longer torn.

Chapter 2

Connor O'Quinn patted his mustache with a napkin, then sat back in his chair, focusing on his wife. "Your cousin is in for a treat," he commented with a smile. "Cooking like that? He'll never leave!"

"Wouldn't that be nice!"

O'Quinn stood, then took his dishes to the sink. "Let's not be hasty, my dear—Decklin may not appreciate our simple means. Our way of life . . ."

"What's not to like," Alannah O'Quinn teased as she stood to give him a kiss before he walked out the door.

"Well, we'll soon find out, won't we?" Returning the smooch, he grabbed his cap from the coat rack. "Hopefully, he'll be on time!"

With that, her husband was gone, leaving her to wonder if they did, indeed, make a mistake when inviting her cousin from the States to spend the summer with them. *He was, after all, a well-respected homicide detective in his country's capitol, and a daily life of fishing may not suit him. But, if it doesn't,* she thought as she rinsed the dishes, *he can always leave . . .*

A thought she didn't wish to entertain.

It had been a long time since Alannah O'Quinn had the opportunity to enjoy her family. Most emigrated to the United States in the early 1900s, and those who chose to remain were less than successful, something always sticking in her American family's craw. By the time of the millennium's turning, Irish roots meant little to them, so it was quite a surprise when her cousin Decklin contacted her about spending a little quality time together.

What he really meant was he needed to get away.

Of course, she didn't ask questions—it wasn't her place. She was raised to stick by those who were blood, never to turn her back on family who may need assistance. God knows she had to call on family more than once during her adult years, so who was she to say no when one of her own came calling?

Still, it was strange.

Awkward? A little. But, by the time Connor and Decklin exchanged handshakes at the Dublin Airport then headed out on the three-hour trip back to Cobh, both felt the energy of a family bond even though Connor was related only by marriage.

"It's beautiful country," Decklin commented as a quaint, yet modern, fishing village appeared on the horizon.

"Indeed, it is!" Connor glanced at his passenger, noticing a touch of sadness in Decklin's eyes. "A wee bit different than what you're used to in the States!"

A smile. "That's an understatement! Where I'm from, places like this don't exist . . ." Another smile. "Is this it? Cobh?"

Connor nodded, then grinned. "The first thing is to pronounce the name right! It's 'Cove'—not 'Cob.'"

A flush creeped into Decklin's cheeks, embarrassed by the fact he didn't even take to the time to learn anything about where his cousin Alannah lived—all he knew and cared about was it was away from D.C. "I guess that would be helpful," he said with a grin.

A brief silence. "So, Mr. Decklin Kilgarry," Connor finally asked, "what brings you to our little village?" A pause. "Although, to be fair, it isn't so little, anymore—nearly eleven thousand people! Thirteen on a good day!"

Kilgarry smiled, thinking how different the next few months would be—with luck, his time in the small fishing village would be just what he needed to retool his perspective on life. "Thirteen thousand? I can't imagine..." Rolling down his window, he focused on the sweet, salty fragrance of the sea air as Connor slowed, then turned onto a narrow street. "Just like the pictures..."

"I thought I'd take you through the town—you know, to get a feel for it since you'll be here awhile!"

So, for the next twenty minutes, Connor drove slowly past areas of interest, pointing out bits of history as they finally made their way to the O'Quinn home. "We're back," he announced as Alannah stood on the front stoop of a modest, tidy, rock home, slipping off her apron and placing it on a chair. "I think she's ready to say hello!"

"Decklin Kilgarry, you're a sight for sore eyes!" Alannah laughed as she ran down the steps, scooping him into one of her village famous bear hugs. Then, she held him at arm's length, appraising him from head to toe. "You look just like Auntie!"

"And, you look just like Uncle Robbie!"

"That's what everyone says!" A pause. "He would've liked your being here..."

"I'm sorry I didn't know him—but, I've heard stories!"

"I'll bet you have!" Alannah, grabbed his hand. "I have lunch ready!"

Connor grinned as he hoisted Decklin's luggage from the car's trunk. "I told you she was ready to say hello!"

Dying flames flickered to embers as the two men sat in front of the fire's warmth, both nursing a coffee and Irish cream. Although Decklin tried to imagine what life in a small fishing village was like, it was nothing like he was experiencing. "How long have you been here," he asked, taking stock of the home's decor.

"Here? Well, ever since Michael died—so, twenty years now, I think is a fair guess." Connor paused for a warming sip. "It's been in the O'Quinn family for centuries, dating back to when Cobh was named Queenstown . . ."

"It suits you."

Connor eyed him. "It does, yes—fishing has been in our family since I can remember. It's what we're born to do . . ."

"So, I'm guessing it's a fair assumption to say you've never thought of doing anything else . . ."

"Anything else? What on God's green earth would I do?" He laughed at the thought of wearing a suit. "I'm not the type of man . . ." Another silence as both men's thoughts took them to private places. "And, what about you, Decklin? I'm never one to pry, but . . ."

"Why am I here?"

"Well, yes—although we've just officially met, it doesn't take a genius to see pain in your eyes. Or, feel the ache in your heart . . ."

A sudden burst of energy from a final flame illuminated the Washington detective's face, revealing the truth of his cousin-in-law's words. Glancing at the man seated beside him, a hand-crafted table between them, he focused on the fading embers. "Well," he began, "I certainly owe you an explanation . . ."

"You owe us nothing—but, if we can help, we will. Alannah's thrilled you're here for any reason . . ."

"I appreciate that—but, I do owe you an explanation." A pause. "One more? This might take a while . . ."

Finn Kildare sat, taking time to meet the eyes of each man seated at the conference table—such that it was. Scratched and marred with decades of life, the farm table his father made now served as a grounding of sorts as the men gathered to discuss what only a few were sanctioned to know. "Progress?"

"Nothing."

"How can there be nothing?"

"That's what we want to know—this lies square on your shoulders, Finn Kildare, and you damned well know it!"

"Is that what you think? All of you? If so, then have the guts to say it!"

Silence.

"Well, then—it seems your opinion is in the minority." He leveled a glare at his opposition, considering his best options. There was little doubt Keegan Sullivan was worth keeping an eye on—dissension among the troops was never a good thing, especially when money was everyone's motivating factor. "If you were in my position, Keegan, what would you do?"

The surly, broad-nosed Irishman stood, the stench of fish an unpleasant plus. "It's not my place, Finn—you speak for us, and we joined you because of a mutual cause!" He paused, thinking of every complaint. "If this situation is allowed to go on?" A glare. "Then, perhaps, we need to regroup . . ."

Kildare said nothing, gauging the reaction of each man at the table. Finally, he spoke. "You are my eyes and ears on the vessels, Gentlemen. I rely on you to bring me information—without knowledge, I can do nothing."

"They're saying nothing," one commented.

"Then, you're not talking to the right people."

Sullivan again sat. "Then, who? Who do we strike up a conversation with as we're slinging fish guts into a pot?"

Finn Kildare's face set, considering the question, wondering if Keegan Sullivan really were that stupid. "You talk to the guy next to you, Keegan—he possesses more information than you think." Again, he eyed each man at the table. "But, we don't care about him—the little guy. It's those at the top capturing our attention."

"We'll never get to the top, Finn! That's what we're trying to say!"

"That may be so." A pause. "But, I will . . ."

Connor stoked the fire, added two more logs, then reclaimed his seat next to Decklin. "Alright—I'm as ready as I'll ever be!"

Taking a sip of a fresh their drinks, Decklin smiled, enjoying the new camaraderie he felt with someone he barely knew. "You may be sorry!"

"I doubt it . . ."

A deep breath. "Well, as you know, I was a cop in Washington D.C. for twenty-five years—maybe a few more, but who's counting?"

"On the street?"

Decklin nodded. "Kind of—after paying my dues, I promoted to detective, and that's what I did for the last couple of decades."

"Homicide?"

"Primarily."

Connor didn't look at him, choosing to keep his attention on the crackling fire. "A lot of pressure for a man . . ."

"Yes—too much, I fear."

"What about your family?" A sip. "How did they deal with your being gone at all hours?"

"At first, it was fine—but, after the kids were off to college, I realized my marriage wasn't what I thought it was."

"Meaning?"

"I guess I wasn't home enough . . ."

Connor placed his coffee mug on the table. "Is that the inference I think it is?"

A nod. "You get the idea . . ."

"Indeed, I do."

Both listened as Alannah finished cleaning up the evening's dishes, then pad softly to the library door. "I'm tired—an early evening for me, I'm afraid!" With that, she wished her husband and Decklin a pleasant evening, knowing darned well she didn't need to be a part of their conversation. "Tomorrow, I'll show you around Cobh!"

"She has more energy in her little finger than I have in my entire body," Decklin commented as they listened to her climb the stairs.

"Aye—she's a good one, that's for sure!"

And, that was that—a confidential moment between two new friends, gone. Was there more to Decklin's story?

Perhaps.

But, Connor O'Quinn wasn't about to ask.

Chapter 3

"Do you fish," Alannah asked as she eased into a parking space in the middle of the village. "I can't imagine a Kilgarry who doesn't!"

"A little—but, not really."

"I'm not sure there is such a thing," Decklin's cousin laughed as she cut the ignition and both climbed out of the car. "But, if there is, I'm sure you know about it!"

Decklin looked both directions, a smile on his lips—it had been quite a while since he felt free enough to laugh. "Which way first?"

Alannah pointed. "That way!"

So, for the next hour they strolled, Alannah chattering about life in the village. "It's not really a village, I suppose—at least, by your standards. But, I prefer to call it that..."

"Why?"

"Because I don't want to see it change."

Decklin stopped, gently taking his cousin's elbow, stepping to the side, allowing people to pass. "Change how?"

Sudden tears filled her eyes. "Didn't Connor tell you?"

"No—tell me what?"

"Our livelihood—it's threatened by illegal fishing. And, from everything we can tell, there's nothing we can do about it..."

"No—he didn't say anything about it."

As if shaking off something she didn't want to think about, Alanna smiled, then grabbed his hand. "Come on! It's time you had some proper fish and chips!"

Keegan Sullivan pulled a cigarette from his pocket, lit it, then enjoyed a long, deep drag. "I don't know why I do this miserable job," he complained. "Don't pay shit—and, I'm working my ass off for what?" He didn't wait for an answer. "Nothin'. Not a damned thing!" From behind his sunglasses, he watched as the new deckhand dumped a bucket of fish guts.

The newbie grinned, flicking his own cigarette with the tip of his finger. "It ain't so bad! But, if you hate it so much, why don't you do something else?"

Keegan spat, then wiped remaining spittle from his chin. "Like what, wise-ass?"

"I don't know—all I know is I'm in it for the money. That's it . . ."

"Same—but, there's something about this whole thing that curdles my gut." It was a direction Keegan didn't necessarily want to go, but, after his conversation with Finn Kildare, he figured Kildare's suggestion was worth a try. "Haven't you felt it?"

The young Spaniard picked up the bucket of guts, dousing his cigarette on the trawler's railing—then, he flicked it into the sea without a thought. "I don't know what you're talking about, man—all I feel is money greasing my palm."

A statement making Keegan Sullivan think twice. In the fishing game since he was a young lad, he knew for a fact most working for the small trawlers didn't refer to receiving wages as 'greasing my palm.' "Well, you must be paid a lot more than me, lad—what's yer secret?"

Sullivan's strong Irish brogue proved difficult for the young Spaniard to understand, but, to be polite, he gave it his best shot. "No secret—it's all about who pays the bills." With that, he kicked the newly emptied bucket of guts into the corner, securing it tightly.

Then, an assessment of the Irishman standing beside him. "You seem like a good guy, Sullivan—if you're interested in an—increase—in wages, maybe you haven't met the right people."

Keegan gasped slightly, hoping the Spaniard didn't notice. "You sayin' you can make that happen?"

A nod. "I'll be in touch . . ."

He checked the guts bucket one more time, then pulled a fresh cigarette from his jacket pocket. "Just be ready . . ."

Finn Kildare kept a wary eye on Sullivan as he listened, knowing how much the man sitting across from him needed progress in his life—any progress. "That's exactly what he said," he asked.

Keegan nodded, then took a long draw on his beer. "His words—I'm waiting for him to get in contact with me."

"You gave him your cell number?"

The gritty fisherman laughed, amused by Kildare's question. "I'm not quite that stupid, Finn—as it happened, I picked up a throwaway just for that purpose. I had me a feelin' . . ."

Kildare finally grinned, certain it was the first good news he received in a long while. "Excellent—what's his name?"

"Guys on the trawler call him 'Smokey.' That's all I know—but, I can tell you he ain't from around here."

"Another country?"

Another nod. "Italy. Spain, maybe . . ."

One more bit of good news? Spanish fishermen were recently arrested by the Irish for poaching salmon. "When's your next shift," he asked, thinking of every possible way Keegan Sullivan could obtain the deckhand's name.

"Tomorrow."

"Will your friend be working?"

"Maybe—you know they come and go."

Kildare was quiet for a few seconds, before suggesting exactly what Sullivan didn't want to hear. "If he's on the trawler tomorrow, I think it's a good idea to make friends, don't you?"

"By doing . . ."

"It's simple—suggest a beer after work."

"You know I don't do well in public . . ."

"Well, this time Keegan, you'll just have to suck it up and find out as much information as you can. You know the saying about 'loose lips' . . ."

Without a word or nod, Keegan Sullivan downed his beer, then headed for the pub door.

Orders clear.

Even though Decklin Kilgarry had been in Ireland for less than a week, a new tradition was quickly born—Alannah would excuse herself, allowing the men to decompress from the long day with a drink and warm fire. No matter the season, there always seemed to be a chill, especially in the evening. "Alannah tells me," he commented, "there's an issue in Cobh regarding illegal fishing . . ."

Connor said nothing for a moment or two. The mere mention of what fishermen were experiencing as the result of ineptitude of local and higher government made him cringe. "It's an assault on our livelihood, Decklin—and, it seems there isn't a damned thing we can do about it."

For the next hour, Connor O'Quinn bared his soul about the stress. Disappointment. Resignation. It seemed no matter how his community tried, there was little to be done about interlopers invading their waters for monetary gain.

"It's not just here," Connor continued. "Canada's eastern shores are struggling with the same thing. Indigenous cultures versus us—the little guys." He paused, renewed frustration creeping into his voice. "Not to mention all the payoffs—rampant corruption, and we're the ones to pay the price."

"I recall there being the same issue—well, sort of—in Washington State years ago, as well."

"I heard about that—in Canada, fishermen are having a dispute over fishing on the East Coast. Indigenous cultures can fish whenever they like and how often they like, paying no attention to how they're depleting jobs." A pause. "And who catches it in the ass?" A brief pause. "Commercial fisherman, that's who—they're starving as a result."

"What about the government?" Decklin regarded the situation in Canada appalling, especially since it was close to his home court.

"The government?" Connor chuckled at the thought. "Maybe they have no idea how to stop it . . ."

"Or, maybe they don't want to—especially if payoffs are involved."

"It's all about regulations—and, a need to stop the poachers and anyone else who's stealing by over-fishing and leaving commercial fisherman without a damned job!"

Well, it's safe to say the whole mess piqued Decklin's interest and curiosity. He'd be lying if he said he didn't miss getting his hands dirty in the bowels of D.C.'s burgeoning, quickly escalating violence. As much as he abhorred the results of such a debacle, it never tainted his desire to do the best he could within the confines of any investigation. "Is there anything I can do to help?"

Connor shook his head. "I doubt it. Besides, you're from away—people would look at you the same way they look at the poachers."

"Even if I call a town meeting, offering my help?"

"You'd do that?"

Decklin smiled, recognizing a flicker of hope in his cousin-in-law's eyes. "And, more—if I can."

For the first time that evening, Connor O'Quinn smiled, relief apparent. "I know just the place—and, there's someone you may want to meet."

"Before the meeting?"

"I think that would be best—his name is Finn Kildare. He's been trying to infiltrate particular poachers for months without luck."

Kilgarry was quiet for a few seconds, thinking about what Connor just told him. "It seems that might be a little risky, don't you think?"

"Hell, yes, it's risky! If he—or, any of his guys—get caught, it's lights out. Poachers won't put up with such a thing, yet who would know if there were a dump out at sea? No one! Not a soul!"

There was little doubt Connor's argument made sense—infiltrating anything was always risky business, and the possibility of leaving a traceable scent was pretty darned high. A risk worth taking?

Decklin wasn't sure.

Keegan Sullivan peeked out the window, not quite ready to endure another day on the trawler, especially in the driving rain. "A day made for the devil, himself," he muttered as he grabbed his slicker and boots.

Then, he checked his phone—nothing.

After his conversation with Smokey, he wasn't sure what to expect. Chances were good the guy was handing him a line of B.S., pulling his chain out of pure amusement. But, the more he thought about it, the more he didn't think so. *Why would he say anything, if he couldn't back it up*, he wondered as he closed the front door behind him, rain splatting against his face the second he stepped outside.

Within twenty, the docks appeared, trawlers and charter boats waiting to make their pennies. Although it was early, tourists strolled the walkways, checking out each fishing vessel, commenting on what they thought of each one. Some boats were, of course, larger than others, some more expensive—but, no matter how they looked, their goals were identical.

Make money.

"What took you so long, Sullivan?" Smokey shot him a grin as he prepared bait for the day.

"I always get here at the same time . . ."

Smokey said nothing, recognizing contempt for their trade in the fisherman's voice. He hadn't contacted Sullivan about introducing him to those who made all decisions, uncertain if the crusty, middle-aged man were worth the trouble—but, there was something about Keegan he liked.

Liking, however, didn't matter.

"Be at Shannon's at seven," Smokey ordered, making a spontaneous decision. "And, don't show up stinkin' like salmon." He glanced at Keegan, then returned to gutting fish. "Don't be late . . ."

"You are not buying," Alannah scolded her cousin as they took a seat at a table close to the pub's front window. "Connor and I won't allow it!"

Decklin smiled, then scanned the small room, taking note of those who seemed out of place—something left over from his detective days. "Then, I pay next time—and, I won't take no for an answer!"

"Deal!" Alannah looked at her cousin, a soft smile on her face. "Are you glad you came to Ireland?"

He sat back in his chair, then placed his menu on the table. "To be honest, I didn't know what to expect—but, the longer I'm here, the more I realize I made the right decision."

"I'm so glad—your being here is good for us, too. It's been a long time since Connor had someone to talk to about his troubles."

"Troubles?"

A nod. "You know—he's been a charter captain for years, and it brought in good money." Alannah paused, thinking about how things used to be. "But, recently? It isn't sustainable . . ."

"You're talking about the poaching . . ."

"Yes—although Connor fishes for everything, charters are his bread and butter." Another pause. "It's not safe, anymore, either—I think it's just a matter of time before things really get out of hand."

Recognizing her stress, Decklin reached over and squeezed her hand. "I'm going to find out as much as I can while I'm here—maybe, there's something I can do."

The thought of a family member whom she barely knew coming to her aid was something she never considered. "Thank you," she said softly, returning the squeeze.

For the first time, Decklin Kilgarry felt a strong family bond.

And, he liked it.

Chapter 4

To many, Shannon's was the quintessential Irish pub—a brawl or two wasn't out of the question, especially when interlopers decided to take matters into their own hands. The place where seasoned fishermen chose to meet, the fragrance of gutted fish was first to greet those brave enough to open the door. Most important? Tourists weren't particularly welcomed.

Keegan checked his watch, questioning whether he made the right decision—tipping a pint with someone he didn't know wasn't his thing, causing him to question ulterior motives. And, when he thought about it, there really wasn't any reason for Smokey to set up a meeting—so, the question became what did he have to gain?

Before he could make a list in his mind, the pub door opened, Smokey and a man he'd never seen before crossing the threshold. A few at the bar turned, casting approving or disapproving glances, while others could've cared less.

"Glad you're on time," Smokey commented as both sat down at Keegan's table. "We only have a few minutes . . ." He paused, assessing Keegan's willingness to talk. "This is Delgado."

A nod instead of a handshake.

"Smokey tells me you're not happy with your current position . . ."

"Happy? Not really—I don't know how happy I can be while I'm fishin' fer no money."

A snort coupled with a long stare. "Well, now—maybe I can help. If it's more money you're after, it seems we have things to discuss."

As he spoke, as much as Keegan tried, he couldn't place the accent. While there was Irish present, he wasn't sure if Delgado were Italian or Spanish. If Spanish, then there might be a tie to the Spaniards who were recently arrested for poaching in Irish waters. "What do you got for me?"

Fifteen minutes later? Still no handshake, but an agreement—one unwise to break. *Kildare's going to love this*, Keegan thought as he paid for his beer, then stepped outside, lighting a cigarette. Zipping up his jacket, he suddenly looked up, alerted by something unfamiliar.

As he squinted into the gauzy, misting, evening light, he saw it—a shadow darting behind the building across the street. *Probably nothin'*, he thought as he headed for home.

Probably nothin', at all . . .

Decklin grinned as he listened to Connor trying to convince Alannah what she was planning for dinner was fine—there would simply be one more mouth at the table. Of course, she didn't mind, and listening to the banter between them reminded Decklin of how things used to be. "Connor O'Quinn," he heard her say, "how dare you invite someone to our table without asking me!"

Then, a big hug.

So, precisely at six-thirty that evening, Connor answered the door, responding to a firm, triple knock. "Finn Kildare! Come in!"

It had been a long time since the two broke bread together. Finn preferred to stay under the radar because of his work, and Connor was okay with it. For both, there was no sense inciting emotions—and, there were plenty of those floating around since the beginning of the summer.

"Decklin Kilgarry, meet Finn Kildare!"

Both men grinned as they shook hands, each feeling an instant camaraderie. "Kilgarry, eh? Not many of you around these parts!"

"I confess I know little about my heritage, or anyone around here other than Alannah and Connor! But, I'm glad to be here, nonetheless . . ."

Just then, Alannah arrived with a smile and a plate of appetizers. "Make yourselves comfortable, gentlemen—dinner will be in half an hour." With that, she returned to the kitchen, leaving the men to eat and discuss—well, things.

"As much as I appreciate the dinner invitation," Kildare began, "I know there's a reason."

Connor nodded, glancing at Decklin. "You know me too well—and, you're right. There is a reason . . ." Again, he glanced at Kilgarry. "Alannah's cousin here has offered to help us with our problem."

Finn's eyes narrowed, slightly uncomfortable with the possible topic of conversation. "And, what problem is that?"

Sensing Kildare's reluctance, Decklin took the lead. "Shortly after I arrived in Cobh, I learned of the illegal poaching issue within Irish waters . . ."

"Aye—it's a problem, that's for sure. It appears there's nothing we can do until we infiltrate the organizations—at the top."

"Government?"

"Completely useless—and, as it stands now, we're losing massive percentages of our catches and income for the current year." He paused, knowing the dangers facing his country. "And, that's not all—illegal commercial poaching is affecting other countries, as well."

Decklin listened, mentally rifling through a list of questions. "Connor told me—do you know who's responsible in Ireland and, specifically in your area?"

"Yes and no—I have suspicions, but it's proving difficult to get any of my men placed in advantageous positions on their boats." He paused, unaware of Keegan Sullivan's recent progress. "I have one man who's knocking at the door, but nothing is confirmed."

"Names?"

"One—Smokey. He currently works on the same boat as my guy."

"No last name?"

Finn shook his head, sighing deeply. "It's impossible to get any information—and, time is running out, I'm afraid. With fish percentages down this year, it may be the last for many of our locals."

Decklin was quiet for a moment, thinking of reasonable possibilities. "What if we draw them out?"

Kildare glanced at Connor, then returned his attention to Decklin. "Explain . . ."

"Well—nothing comes to the surface unless it's forced, so how about a town meeting? It's a sure bet once Smokey and his group hear of it, someone will be there."

"More than one, I'd say . . ."

A nod. "Yes. But, so will I . . ."

By the end of his first month in Cobh, Decklin Kilgarry felt like one of the locals—to the point, in fact, he considered renting a quaint, seaside home just down the road from the O'Quinns. "I just saw the sign today," Alannah mentioned as she peeled potatoes for a hearty breakfast. "And, the rent seems right . . ."

Decklin sipped his coffee, listening with one ear. It was an interesting idea, one he hadn't considered—yet, if he could rent it for a short period of time, it might be worth exploring. "Let me think about it," he finally commented. "But, I will say I'm tempted!"

Alannah turned to him. "It's perfect, Decklin—it's white and the outside needs works, but the inside is wonderful! I've been in it a few times, and it suits you."

And, so it did.

By the end of the week, Decklin Kilgarry became an unofficial resident of Cobh, County Cork, Ireland. Alannah was right—after stepping across the threshold of his new cottage for the first time, he knew he made the right decision.

He was home.

As intriguing as Decklin's idea of a town meeting was, it didn't take Finn Kildare long to realize it could work—or, backfire. "Locals don't know who you are," he commented. "You're from away, and no one is going to trust you . . ."

"It's as I said, Decklin—townsfolk don't appreciate people poking their noses into their business." Connor paused. "If this plan is to work, you say nothing . . ."

Kildare agreed. "If Connor simply introduces you as his cousin..."

"And," Kilgarry noted, "that allows me the opportunity to observe. My years as a detective will come in handy..."

Connor glanced at Finn, still unsure if the risk were worth taking. "Exactly what does that mean, Decklin?"

"Well, a lot of things, really—for one, while discussion is going on, I can pay attention to those who are talking, as well as those who say nothing." He paused as he chose an appetizer from the plate Alannah left on the table. "You know—micro-gestures. Voice inflection. Non-participation."

"What will you be looking for?"

"Duplicity. It always gives itself away..."

So, for the rest of the evening, the men discussed possibilities while Alanna kept to herself until she claimed an early bedtime. Was it something she wanted to do? Of course not—she wanted to know everything. She knew better, however, than to insert herself in such a conversation.

Besides, her husband would tell her all she needed to know.

Wingo watched Sullivan and Smokey with an occasional side glance, her gut telling her something was up. *Keegan Sullivan doesn't talk to anyone,* she thought as she prepared the nets for the next day's catch. If she noticed Sullivan's chattiness only once, that would've been one thing. But, several times? *Something to look into...*

"Sullivan! Get over here!" She stood by the nets, her strong hands checking for compromised knots. Again, from the corner of her eye, she watched as Keegan Sullivan rolled his eyes then flicked his partially smoked cigarette, crushing it into the deck with his foot. Then, he picked it up, tossing it into a large can. "Sullivan!"

Saying nothing, within a few seconds he stood beside her, clearly not in the mood for conversation. "What did I do this time?"

"Nothing, Sullivan—I need you on nets." An untruth, of course, but her gut also told her it was wise to break up any allegiance that may be brewing. There was something about Smokey she didn't trust and—in her mind, Sullivan was stupid enough to fall for anything the deckhand said.

"Permanently?"

"Aye—you're the only man I trust with the knots." It was true, too—Keegan Sullivan was known throughout the village as the best knotter within miles when he wasn't drunk.

Not particularly pleased with his new assignment, Keegan glanced at Smokey who refused to look. There was, however, nothing he could do—Wingo McNamara was one of the toughest bosses of all trawlers, her family having been in the business for decades. Learning the way of the sea by the time she hit first grade, her father made certain to raise a girl who could take care of herself.

And, the family business.

By evening, a raging summer storm docked all boats and trawlers, crews choosing favorite pubs to drown their disappointment—no fishing, no money.

At Shannon's, Delgado threw a flier on the table, disgust apparent. "A town meeting?"

Smokey said nothing, letting the news sink in. After Sullivan's reassignment on the trawler, things seemed to be tipping in a direction neither expected. "Saturday night . . ." he finally answered.

"What do they expect to achieve?"

"Who knows? It doesn't say—but, you can bet everyone in this town will show up for it! And, if Connor O'Quinn is involved, it sure as hell isn't good."

A nod. "I hear he has company . . ."

"I don't know, but O'Quinn's sure to be squawking about our particular line of business."

"Then find out . . ."

"About what?"

Delgado's eyes narrowed. "Who's visiting O'Quinn."

"That shouldn't be too hard," Smokey grinned. "But, anything beyond his name is a different story . . ."

"Then send in Sullivan—he's been itching to make more money. Contact him, and let him know he'll be paid to report back to you about the meeting."

"You're not going?"

As much as Delgado wanted to attend, he knew better. "No," he answered shaking his head. "It's better we send in someone they won't suspect."

"What if . . ."

The man calling the shots focused on his underling with an irritated glare. "It's your job to make it happen." Another glare, just for good measure. "Is there a problem, Alvera?"

Of course, there wasn't.

Chapter 5

Although Cobh wasn't the smallest village, finding the appropriate venue to host a town meeting didn't progress as smoothly as the O'Quinns hoped. Most were too small while proprietors of others didn't want to be a part of it, knowing things may suddenly turn—and, filing insurance claims wasn't on their lists of things to do.

No matter.

Finally, a local farmer offered his land on a lovely summer evening, it seemed the perfect choice—fewer ways to get hurt when landing on fertile soil.

Unfortunately, however, no one wanted to be screaming their lungs out while trying to discuss matters at hand, so Connor finally decided on an abandoned movie theatre forced to close its doors months earlier. The good news? Plenty of seating. The bad news?

Anyone could be watching.

A plus in Connor's mind, nooks and crannies were the reason he chose the theater in the first place. Corners and shadows offered a natural ambiance, including perfect places to lurk. Decklin could slip in through the back, or he could be front and center with those who were interested—either way was fine with him as long as he had the opportunity to observe.

"Only a few know you're here," Connor noted as they tested the sound from an archaic microphone. "Like Finn said—you're from away, and that causes a natural distrust."

Decklin tapped the mic. "Testing, testing . . ." Turning up the volume slightly, he tried again. Finally, he faced Connor. "I can position myself in the wings . . ." He pointed. "That allows me to move forward slowly—by then, I suspect everyone will be riled up enough not to notice."

"Aye—riled, they will be. That's why I wanted Alannah to stay home!"

"She's not coming?"

O'Quinn laughed. "Oh, no—she's coming!"

Kilgarry smiled, enjoying the glint in Connor's eyes. "And, that's the way it should be . . ."

"Are you talking about me," a voice from the rear of the theater called. "You might want to turn off the mic!" She was pretty sure she noticed both men sporting a lovely blush as she headed toward them.

Decklin grinned, then gave her his customary peck on the cheek. "I'm going to get in place," he suggested. "I'll be watching—and, listening."

"Just in time, too . . ." Alannah pointed to the rear of the theater. "You're going to have quite a crowd!" She watched as her cousin took his place in the wings, knowing he could exit and come in through the main or backstage entrance.

Moments later, the heavy doors swung open as villagers headed for seats in the front, only a few hanging back—and, within fifteen, Connor stepped up to the mic. "Thank you for coming," he greeted, his voice strong and sure. "We have much to discuss, so let's get to it! But, orderly—I don't want to pay for damage!" He smiled, hoping to lighten the mood.

Didn't work.

Within minutes, escalating anger seeped through each row with the intention of a snake on the hunt, ready to strike at precisely the right moment. "If we band together, what are they going to do," a man in the back shouted. "Strike back? That's bullshit, and you know it!"

Decklin listened as inflammatory, vigilante rhetoric surged, tension in the theater thickening with each violent suggestion. Then, as Mary Drucine McGregor stood to let everyone know what was on her mind, he noticed a shadow in the wings, stage left. With house lights on, it was difficult to see into the darkness, but, there was one thing he knew for sure. *If I can see him*, he thought, *he sure as hell can see me* . . .

Instinctively, he stepped further back into the shadows, listening to each villager state his or her piece, keeping his eyes on what could be something . . .

Or, nothing.

Quietly, he headed into the depths of the stage-right wings, knowing he'd lose sight of anyone for several moments, save those who may be grabbing a bit of fresh air or a smoke.

Emerging again on the opposite side, he stopped at the backstage entrance, listening. Mary Drucine was still droning on about how unfair it all was, her disgust diminished only by a few disgusting sailors hacking and coughing within an inch of their lives. Then, as he stepped closer to the stage, another movement—only quicker, as if suddenly discovered.

"Ain't you Connor O'Quinn's kin," a voice suddenly whispered from behind his left ear.

Decklin turned, stunned to see no one. *What the . . .* Again, he turned his attention to the main stage. *Maybe it was nothing,* he thought. Then again?

Maybe it was something . . .

Precisely at ten-fifteen, Connor dismissed the meeting, promising those who were still listening that something would be done. By that time, roiling anger settled to a simmer, some feeling spent of energy and emotion, others willing to consider another round.

As it turned out, Decklin stayed within the shadows, comfortable with his position to observe without observation. Whatever voice he heard, he ultimately concluded it was nothing more than imagination, allowing him the comfort of thinking he wasn't out of his mind.

"For the most part," Connor commented as they walked toward Decklin's cottage, "they were pretty well-behaved!" He grinned as he grabbed his wife's hand, helping her across the street.

"Yes, they were . . ."

"Who stood out?"

Decklin thought for a moment. "No one, really . . ." Then, he recalled the voice. "I thought I heard someone directly behind me, but, when I turned around, no one was there."

"I heard that theater is haunted," Alannah exclaimed, the thought of experiencing such a thing more than titillating.

"Oh, stop," Connor chided. "It was probably the sea breeze!" He paused, thinking. "Someone likely left a door open . . ."

"You're right," Decklin agreed, as they reached his gate. "Pretty sure it wasn't a ghost . . ."

"But . . ."

Gently guiding her toward their own home, he winked at his wife's cousin. "Let's go, my dear . . ."

With that, the newcomer to Cobh bid them goodbye, eager to settle in for the evening.

Easier said.

The more he played the meeting's events in his mind, the more he realized something was missing—and, it wasn't until he was ready to watch a bit of television sipping a cup of tea did he realize exactly what it was. No one caught his eye for a reason . . .

Duplicity.

Everyone in the theater, he realized, *was comfortable with everyone else. No one protested villagers' views . . .*

Even though he was new to Ireland, human behavior was basically the same no matter the location. And, in a town meeting?

Definitely the place for dissent.

"Well?"

Keegan Sullivan drained his pint, then swiped at his mouth with his sleeve. "Well, what?"

Dominic Delgado's eyes narrowed as he realized the Irish fisherman was beginning to become a pain in the ass, his first assignment offering less than a positive impression. "The meeting, Sullivan—what happened at the meeting?"

Of course, Keegan knew he was getting on Delgado's last nerve, and it was something the Irishman truly enjoyed. It was his natural way to be obstinate and oblique whenever possible, leaving most who had the unfortunate pleasure to cross his path wishing they turned the opposite direction.

Attributes Delgado admired and required.

"It was too damned long!"

Smokey glanced at his boss, feeling Delgado's seething anger inch uncomfortably closer, knowing to keep his mouth shut—if there were something Delgado hated, it was being interrupted.

Dominic said nothing, waiting.

"Nothing happened," Sullivan finally volunteered. "Connor O'Quinn ran the show, and people said how they felt—that was it."

"Was there anyone with him?"

"O'Quinn?"

"Yes, Sullivan—O'Quinn."

"Nope—no one but that mouthy wife of his." He paused. "She's always talkin' . . ."

A narrowing glare. "That's it? That's your report?"

Sullivan stood, pitching enough Euros on the table to cover his tab. "That all I got—I told you it was as tame as my dear mother's tea. I can't make it anything it wasn't . . ."

Then?

Out the door.

Chapter 6

*W*ords on villagers' lips the morning after the town meeting? "Murder? In Cobh? It simply can't be!"

But, it was.

As you can imagine, it didn't take long for gossip to travel and, by the time trawlers docked to offload daily catches, there wasn't a soul in town who didn't hear the news.

"I heard! Who would do such a thing," Alannah exclaimed when Connor called her from the dock. "He was an odd man, but he didn't deserve this!" Tears welled, knowing their little village shifted from a certain innocence to something dark. Something unknown.

Something unthinkable.

"Does Decklin know?"

"I'll stop by his place on the way home . . ." He paused, his mind asking the obvious. "He was at the meeting . . ."

"Decklin? I know . . ."

"No—Sullivan."

Alannah gasped, realizing what her husband was intimating. "This couldn't have had anything to do with the town meeting—everyone there minded their Ps and Qs, and I certainly didn't notice Keegan getting out of hand!"

With quick agreement as well as a promise to be home by seven, Connor rang off, eager to have a sit down with Alannah's cousin. *If anyone can shed light on such a thing,* he thought as he headed toward Decklin's place, *a Kilgarry can . . .*

It was true—although Connor didn't know much about Decklin's heritage other than how he was related to his wife, it was common knowledge the Kilgarry clan preferred the right side of the law. With more than a few serving their villages or towns as constables and guards throughout the centuries, many were recognized for their community contributions. *With that running through his blood,* he thought as he opened the gate to Decklin's new home, *he sure as hell can figure out who murdered Keegan Sullivan—the poor sot!*

"Why aren't you home having dinner," Decklin asked with a smile as he held the porch door open, surprised when Connor knocked loudly.

"On my way! But, I have something to discuss if you can

spare a minute or two..."

By the sound of Connor's voice, there was little doubt his cousin's husband had something on his mind. "Make yourself at home," he suggested. "Drink?"

Connor nodded. "Aye! It's been a hell of a day..." He waited until Decklin poured a single malt scotch. "Always been a Glenfiddich man, myself," he commented as he handed Kilgarry his glass.

"Agreed. Livet is a little too much citrus..."

Silence as both took a first sip.

Finally, Connor spoke, his voice quiet. Serious. "We have ourselves quite a mess, Decklin. You probably heard..."

"Sullivan?"

Another nod. "He was at the meeting."

Decklin was quiet for a moment, thinking of possible ramifications. "Do you think his murder has anything to do with the town meeting?" Of course, he could've addressed Connor's assertion immediately—it was far wiser, however, to listen before offering an opinion or solution.

"I don't know—but, it seems like a hell of a coincidence to me."

"Well, that's a possibility." A pause. "The question is why Sullivan? As I recall, there were only a few people who really spoke out, and he wasn't one of them."

"Alannah said the same thing—and, I didn't see anyone who shouldn't have been there." A sip. "But, my gut tells me things are going to get ugly..."

Kilgarry said nothing, his gut telling him the same thing. "What can I do?"

Connor shook his head. "Damned if I know! But, I can tell you our little village isn't equipped for this . . ." Swishing the scotch in his glass, he thought of his wife. "It's this kind of thing that can shut us down permanently" he finally commented. "How do you do it?"

"Not sure I follow—do what?"

"Conduct an investigation—as much as I respect our local guards, they don't have what it takes to solve a murder. Especially one rooted in poaching . . ."

"You think that's what this is about?"

A nod. "I know it is—that's why we need someone of your caliber to guide us." Connor glanced at Decklin, then returned his attention to his drink. "So, I ask again—how do you go about investigating something like this?"

"Well, as odd as it may seem, every investigation follows the same trajectory. It's a process, one that seldom changes according to circumstance . . ." He paused, briefly recalling his last murder case in D.C. "The basic procedure for homicide investigations is the same regardless of the type involved."

"Meaning?"

"From assessing the scene upon arrival—searching, sketching, and documenting—after all of that, it's on to post-scene responsibilities." Pausing, he realized explaining methods of a crime scene investigation wasn't easy. "No matter how complicated or seemingly obvious a case may be, good detectives always approach the investigation in the same methodical way."

"Even in a different country?"

Decklin nodded. "It doesn't make any difference—it's always the same. Timeline is an essential part of every homicide investigation, and it opens investigative avenues."

"What if you get it wrong?"

"Avenues close, proving or breaking a suspect's alibi. Learning everything there is to know about a victim's final days and weeks allows investigators to get to know the victim, his or her habits, friends, and hobbies."

"How long does that take?"

Decklin shrugged. "Depends—but, there's little doubt a thorough investigation can be the difference between a solved case and a cold one."

"What if you don't have any leads?"

"Well, that rarely happens—that's not to say, however, leads don't dry up. That said, keeping an open mind about causes and possible perpetrators of a crime is essential to an investigator's success."

"I'm not sure I can keep an open mind about this . . ."

Both men were quiet, each considering Keegan Sullivan's life in Cobh—and, even though Decklin didn't know him, there was a sense of kinship.

"Most homicides," Decklin finally continued, "are rarely straightforward and following every lead—no matter how contrived they seem—is crucial. Whether it's witness statements or tips called in by the public, detectives never know where a lead is going to take them."

Connor sighed as he drained his drink. "I don't know how our own will take to your help—they may well think you're sticking your nose where it doesn't belong."

"Honestly, I'd probably think the same thing—so, if I'm to be of any help, I suggest we keep it between us."

"Alannah?"

"Of course—but, I have to be honest. Even though the crime is fresh, I'll be at a disadvantage."

"Meaning?"

"Well, for one, I won't have the luxury of being at the crime scene, and that's a problem. Everything at a crime scene—from the victim's body to the position of furniture—can be considered evidence." He paused. "Systematically processing the scene can dramatically increase the chances of solving the crime."

"What about evidence? You won't have access to that, either."

"Agreed. So, I'll need someone to be my ears and eyes when it comes to knowing what local authorities know."

"I think I can arrange that . . ."

"It's not easy, Connor, unless you're on really good terms with whomever is heading up the investigation. You have to remember it's not only about collecting forensic evidence and fingerprints." Again, he paused. "Can you get eyes on the crime scene?"

"Maybe—why?"

"Determining what does or doesn't belong at a scene can be just as useful as DNA or a murder weapon—and, if you're granted access, spend a little more time than a few minutes. I can tell you what to look for . . ."

"I'm sure I can see it—but, it's been twelve hours since poor Keegan's body was discovered down by the docks."

"I know—but, that doesn't mean you can't see things previously unnoticed."

"What should I look for?"

"Anything that could possibly be a murder weapon. You also need to look for blood—whether it's the victim's or attacker's. A tough call when mixed with fish guts . . ."

"I imagine that's already been discovered."

"Probably, but that's okay. There's also gunshot residue—if a gun were used, powder burns are important. So is DNA that isn't the victim's . . ."

"Why is that?"

"Because you can eliminate those people as suspects later. Remember, things pointing to motive can get complicated." Decklin focused on Connor, his voice serious. "For example, if the victim—in this case, Keegan Sullivan—were into illegal activity, this can get very complicated. Finger prints. Lipstick stains. You know what I mean . . ."

Connor nodded, but said nothing, knowing he wouldn't have access to anything Decklin just said. All Connor had going for him?

Talking with those in the know over a pint or two.

"In the beginning of an investigation, no piece is too small, and things are eliminated as the investigation progresses," Decklin continued.

"Is it true the probability of solving a murder is greatest within twenty-four hours?"

A nod. "Yep—and, don't forget there are interviews with neighbors, coworkers, teachers, students or classmates, apartment managers, boyfriends or girlfriends, friends, and family. Anyone who knew the victim . . ."

"As far as I know, Keegan Sullivan was a solitary soul. Preferred a life of drink rather than the comfort of a good woman."

"That may be—but, what goes on behind closed doors is anyone's guess. That's why every bit of evidence paints a picture of the victim that helps put things you find at the scene and victim's home in context." Decklin, too, drained his glass. "Context is important if you're going to figure out who could've wanted Sullivan dead—and, why. Sometimes it's obvious, other times it's like trying to find a needle in a haystack."

"Or, worse. A needle in a stack of needles . . ."

Wingo pushed her plate away, lighting a cigarette to signal dessert was in order, never mind others were still eating. It was a trait most who knew her abhorred, but, honestly, no one dared to mention such poor manners.

And, the truth was they didn't really care.

"Whoever did this will pay," she whispered, mostly to herself.

"What the hell do you care? He was nothin' but a miserable drunk!"

"Maybe—but, now I'm in a position of bringing in someone else on nets."

Her father glared at her, his eyes narrowing in disgust. "A man's been murdered, girl—show proper respect. He was one of ours, no matter what you may think . . ."

"My ass—Keegan Sullivan wasn't worth the ground he walked on, and no one will tell you any different, Dadaí!"

Aidan McNamara stood, slamming his hand on the wooden table. "How dare you speak to me in such a manner! Get out!"

Wingo stood, anger seething. "It's about time someone told you the truth!"

"Get out!"

Without another word, Wingo McNamara grabbed her smokes, hat, and coat, then headed for the door. Suddenly, she turned, her face florid with fear masquerading as something more sinister. "When we meet on the street, pay me no mind—for, as of now, we are strangers."

The door squeaked loudly as she jerked it open with obstinate resolve. *No one will speak to me that way*, she fumed as her boots hit the street.

No one . . .

After Connor left for his wife and a bit of home cooking, it took about five seconds for Decklin to kick into high gear. Doubting whether he should get involved, all thoughts were put to rest as he pulled a legal tablet from a small desk drawer—it wasn't the first time he started without information and he knew, once Connor inserted himself into the investigation, there'd be more. For the moment, however, all he had to go on was recalling Keegan Sullivan at the town meeting the previous evening.

Stripping the cap from a Sharpie fine point, he drew a line from top to bottom in the middle of the page. *Okay—what do I know?*

So, there he sat for the next two hours, scribbling notes about a case of which he knew nothing . . .

And, it felt good.

Chapter 7

Unfortunately, things didn't quite go as planned—Connor O'Quinn mistakenly counted on false allegiances, rendering him completely impotent when it came to gathering useful information. It was, in fact, the opposite—no one was talking and that, in itself, was interesting, if not revealing.

Of course, that's the way it should be—at least, it was in the States. In Ireland?

Not so much.

According to Connor, it wasn't like anyone in town to shut up about anything, and a murder of one of their own would certainly be fodder for corner-store gossip. Even so, as days passed, there was barely a peep about discovering poor

Keegan Sullivan's killer. Words were so silent, in fact, it made one wonder if there were a reason for locked lips.

No one was talking about that, either.

The sad fact was life didn't come to a halt just because Sullivan met his maker. Wingo McNamara was one man down on her trawler, and finding a suitable replacement proved as difficult as anticipated. With fishing season well underway, most capable hands were already working and greenhorns, in her estimation, didn't know crap.

There was, however, a solution she preferred not to consider—secret, circulating word on the docks indicated there was always an answer in difficult times, especially for the right buyer. Although Wingo was in the same financial situation as everyone else in the village, the thought occurred to her it was time for desperate measures as her father often claimed.

Mistake number one.

For someone unfamiliar with society's underbelly, finding alternative solutions wasn't exactly a snap. Infiltrating the unknown usually proved hazardous, but, when opportunities presented themselves?

Wingo was willing try anything once.

As it turned out, she didn't have to go far to find a necessary introduction—Smokey was on it the second Sullivan's body was discovered pinned against a pier. "What will you do now," he asked, eyeing Wingo's work as she repaired the nets in the morning mist. As he saw it, there was no doubt Sullivan's absence would be detrimental to profits—he also knew sailors worth their salt were few and far between.

"I can't think about that now," she commented, refusing to look at him. "There's a lot of work to be done . . ."

With that, Smokey grabbed one of the nets, deftly untying and repairing two knots adjacent to each other. "I know someone . . ."

Well, that presented a predicament. As much as her gut told her to steer clear, finances required a different response. "Who?"

Smokey glanced at her deckhands as they prepared traps at the far end of the trawler, then resumed working on the nets closer to them. "A friend."

Seconds later, he manned his position at the bait buckets, smiling slightly at his good fortune. The more Delgado could infiltrate local business, the easier life would be. *More money for me,* Smokey thought as he flung guts, fish heads, and carcasses into a sack, tying it to the nets.

After all, that was the point, wasn't it?

Still, there was much to be done before Dominic Delgado rose to the heights of his own imagination. *They won't know what hit 'em,* Smokey laughed to himself, thinking of the promises Delgado made when inviting him into the fold. He glanced at Wingo, then made a promise to himself. *By this time next year . . .*

If it weren't for the fact salmon poaching was constantly in the news throughout fishing towns and villages, Keegan Sullivan's unfortunate demise wouldn't have raised an eyebrow. As it was, there was interest—not a lot, but interest just the same.

Two from Ireland's Special Detective Unit—who obviously drew the short straw—showed up in Cobh two weeks later, curious about prevailing circumstances concerning poor Keegan's death. "I doubt there's much to learn," Connor noted as he and Decklin reviewed notes from previous weeks.

"Well, they're here for a reason . . ."

Connor tossed his pen on the table, then sat back in his chair. "There's nothing. Absolutely nothing—and, I don't mind tellin' ya, Decklin, for this village? It ain't right . . ."

Kilgarry was quiet, his gut telling him Connor needed to work through something.

"And, for Sullivan to be found at the docks," Connor continued, "I think whomever did Keegan in was passing a message."

Conjecture laced with merit.

Even though the men were conducting individual, under-the-radar investigations, there was little time to compare notes, especially in the middle of salmon season. "Go on," Decklin prompted, eager to hear what O'Quinn had to say.

"Everybody knows Keegan Sullivan was a drunk—it was a damned miracle he showed up to work on a regular basis." He hesitated for a moment, thinking. "And, when I think about it? It's damned strange Wingo McNamara would put up with him..."

"Who's Wingo McNamara?"

"Aidan McNamara's spawn..."

Decklin smiled, pleased Connor considered him enough of a local to forget Decklin had no idea who was who in the small village. "And, he is?"

Smile returned. "His family's been here since the beginning—hard-working folk, but Aidan's known for getting his way. No matter what..."

"What about Wingo?"

"His daughter? Tough as nails with the mouth of a sailor."

Decklin thought for a minute, working through possibilities regarding the Special Detective Unit's surprise appearance. "Do you know if they were called in?"

"The detectives?" Connor shook his head. "I don't think so—I saw them with the locals heading up the investigation when they were at the docks this morning, and they didn't look any too pleased."

"The local guys?"

"Aye. I've known most on our police force for years—well enough to recognize a disgusted look on their faces—and, today?" Connor grunted. "Disgust doesn't describe it..."

"Did you notice who they were talking to," Decklin asked, hoping Connor recalled their conversation about investigative procedure.

Again, Connor shook his head. "I tried, but I had work to do . . ."

"Do you know if they spoke with Wingo?"

A nod. "When we pulled away from the dock, I saw them boarding her trawler." A pause. "Obviously, I have no idea what was said . . ."

A brief silence. "Is there any way," Decklin finally asked, "you can introduce me to Wingo McNamara?"

Connor's eyes narrowed. "Why?"

"I don't know—but, my gut tells me she has something interesting to say." Another silence. "Well?"

"Maybe—on Fridays, she's known to be at Shannon's after she comes off the water."

"Drinking with the boys?"

A nod. "Or, by herself . . ."

Losing an informant is never a good thing, but, as Finn Kildare considered a reasonable replacement, he quickly realized there was none—a situation making his job more difficult.

Not impossible, however.

Word circled there was a young greenhorn looking for work, but, at that point in the season, few trawlers were willing to take on someone with little experience. As far as he knew, Wingo McNamara was still looking, but hadn't hired—a fact he found interesting. Still, there was much to be said for a well-placed interception—if he offered enough, he had no doubt such a young man might be the injection his investigation needed.

"What do you bring to the table," he asked, keeping an eye on his target.

"I fished last year—but, we were shut down because of poachers."

Finn nodded. "So, you're looking for a job, are ya?"

"Yes, Sir."

It was then Finn Kildare made a snap decision. "You a good listener?"

Rowan Murphy pulled back slightly, curious what listening had to do with fishing. "I guess so . . ."

Finn said nothing for a moment, weighing what he was about to say. "I can offer work—but, it may not be what you have in mind."

Of course, Kildare was taking a monumental risk by trusting someone he barely knew—but, what choice did he have? Besides, Murphy was young enough for Finn to carve him into exactly what he needed.

The question was did he have time . . .

Within rays of a setting sun, trawlers docked one-by-one, their catches less than impressive. Boats finally moored, deckhands headed for their favorite watering holes, Wingo McNamara leading the charge to put another week's work in the books. Only the most hardcore headed for Shannon's, most fearing they'd have to listen to Wingo rail on about social injustices in Cobh, and Ireland in general. Still, as much as they hated her soapbox?

She was right.

It was a situation getting worse by the day, no one blaming her for releasing her pressure-cooker steam. A few pints in?

She'd say anything.

"I told them exactly what I knew about Keegan Sullivan," she roared, aware of a blooming, florid flush. "He was a no good drunk!" She paused, glaring at each deckhand at her table, pitifully unaware of the irony. "So, why the hell are they so interested in a guy who was drunk on his ass, and fell in?"

Of course, no one answered—but, her questions did cause a few who might be listening to answer them to themselves. The fact no one batted an eye when word circulated of Sullivan's last dive into the drink was interesting in itself—but, for big guns to show up out of nowhere? Asking questions?

Well, it was a bit odd.

Dominic Delgado watched as he sat in the corner, considering whether Wingo McNamara may be interested in what he was about to offer. There was, naturally, a chance misguided and misplaced allegiance to her village and family may take precedence, but, knowing her financial situation?

He doubted it.

As his boss continued her tirade, Smokey glanced at the corner, leaving no impression of previous communication—he was there only for backup, should the need arise.

Finally, as doors closed for the night, Delgado offered a helping hand as Wingo tried to make it to the entrance without landing on her ass. "I can help you home," he offered as they stepped into an uncustomary, frigid drizzle.

An unfamiliar voice snapped her back to partial sobriety, if only for a moment. "Who are you?"

"A friend . . ."

Quickly, she jerked her arm from his grasp. "Who the hell are you?"

"Please—Wingo. I'm not your enemy—in fact, I'm the answer to your prayers . . ."

Even in her inebriated state, the hair on Wingo's arms stood at attention as she inconspicuously placed her fingertips on the knife she used to cut nets.

A gesture not unnoticed.

Just then, Smokey rounded the side of the building, catching Delgado's glance, warning him to stay back. "I know you need a good hand, and I know someone who's looking for a job . . ."

"Who? Do I know him?"

A smile. "I doubt it—but, I assure you, he's very good at what he does."

Suddenly, Wingo blanched, then puked. "Can he knot," she finally asked, swiping at her mouth with her jacket sleeve stained from fish.

"I'm sure he can . . ." Delgado waited a moment. "Are you feeling better?"

She nodded. "When can he start?"

"Is tomorrow soon enough?"

Another nod. "Daybreak. At the docks . . ." With that, she straightened herself, unaware of newly planted stains on her coat.

"I'll tell him," Delgado answered with a smile. "I'm sure he'll work out just fine . . ."

For Wingo?

Mistake number two.

Chapter 8

Whenever family dissension slowly surfaces, it allows for a certain acceptance of the conflicting situation. When it boils over like a pot of potatoes?

Trouble.

Of course, Aidan McNamara knew he played a part, opting for the iron fist rather than the velvet glove when raising his daughter. But, when thinking about it, was there really an alternative?

He didn't think so.

Was he harsh? Yes. Did he care?

Not really.

It wasn't his fault he didn't get what he wished for, but he'd be damned if he didn't try his best to raise an heir to his paltry fortune. Family tradition was his world, and tossing it aside simply wasn't acceptable—something sticking in his independent daughter's craw.

Legs stretched in front of him, he sat on his favorite seaside bench, clutching a mug of coffee as dawn promised to warm the day. The chaos with Wingo left a bitter and sour taste—one he didn't particularly enjoy—yet, he knew it was up to him to mend fences. All of them. Thinking about it, his daughter's lack of an acceptable personality was his doing. From the time she was old enough to understand, he felt it prudent to rid her of pesky traces of nonconformity when it came to family tradition.

Since she was born, Aidan promised to make her a fisherman—never mind her gender—taking her on the family trawler from the time she could walk. By the time she was ten, her little fingers nimbly untied and repaired the nets, always holding them up for parental approval when the task was done. *She was hopeful, I suppose*, he considered as he recalled prior decades.

Hopeful, indeed.

Not a day went by without seeking her father's approval about something—and, not a day went by when he refused. Praise? Surely, Wingo didn't expect that . . .

But, she did.

So, from an early age, she learned to steel herself against disappointment, knowing all she truly had was her own sense of importance—and, it was then she began to live life as she saw fit—outside of family confines.

Something her father abhorred.

"I heard you need a hand . . ." Sean Braniff called from the dock, hoping to gain someone's attention. "Permission to come aboard?"

Nothing.

Suddenly, a voice from the wheelhouse. "Who the hell are you?" Obviously, Wingo McNamara didn't quite recall her conversation with Dominic Delgado the prior evening.

"Sean Braniff, Ma'am."

"Don't all me that," she answered, disapproving disdain obvious. "What do you want?"

"I heard you need a deckhand!"

Opening the small window completely, she eyed him, refusing to extend the courtesy of inviting him aboard. "Maybe." A pause. "Let's talk . . ."

Of course, it didn't dawn on Wingo it was her lucky day until a second voice hailed her from the dock minutes after Sean Braniff stepped onto the trawler. "Wingo McNamara?"

Again, she popped her head out of the tiny wheelhouse's sliding window. "Who the hell are you?"

Listening carefully to his answer, even in her slightly hungover state it quickly became clear her prayers were answered. "Come aboard . . ."

So, seconds later, there she stood, two strong, young men standing in front of her asking for a job.

It was, indeed, her lucky day.

Decklin admired the colorful homes as he headed toward the village library, enjoying the fragrance of the seaside town. It had been a long time since he felt so free, not guilty one little bit about how things turned out. *It was meant to be*, he thought as he pulled on the Cobh Library door. Why he was there he wasn't exactly sure—but, years of detective experience told him to follow his gut. Three hours later?

More than he expected.

Finally stepping into a late afternoon rain, he tapped his cell. "Are you available tonight," he asked.

Moment's later, he clicked off, the remaining hours of his day set.

Things are getting interesting . . .

"I called in a few favors," Decklin commented as he poured two single malts, then handed one to Connor. "And, thanks for stopping by on your way home, by the way . . ." He grinned, then raised his glass in a toast. "May our days take us where we want them to go . . ."

Connor laughed, lifting his glass. "I take it from that look on your face, we have something to discuss." A pause. "Something I want to hear, I hope." A longer pause. "So—don't keep a tired fisherman waiting!"

Decklin took his usual seat, then a slow sip. "I went to the library today . . ."

"The library? Good Lord, why? It's been years since I set foot in there!"

"Well, at first, I wasn't sure—but, when I opened the door, it felt like home." He glanced at Connor. "I know it sounds strange, but it was a feeling I couldn't ignore, so I did a little research . . ."

"What kind of research?"

"Family—turns out, the Kilgarry clan enjoyed solving a good mystery."

"That's true—but, that's all I know. Alanna doesn't talk about her heritage much, and I suspect there's a reason for it. But, I don't pry . . ."

Decklin nodded. "I noticed the same thing."

Both were quiet for a moment or two, each wondering about things Alannah didn't want either to know. "So, what did you learn," Connor finally asked.

"Well—it was interesting to learn about my family, of course, but it was something else catching my eye."

"And, that was . . ."

"A family feud."

Connor laughed, then took another sip. "Aye—all families have them, I'm afraid!"

"Agreed—this feud, though, was with the Kilgarrys. Apparently, my ancestors were known for bringing criminals to justice, no matter who they were."

Placing his glass on the side table, Connor smiled. "Sounds like quite a tale . . ."

"It was—enough of one to cause a permanent chasm between the Kilgarrys and the Murphys. Although, murder tends to do that, I suppose . . ."

"Murder?"

A nod. "Right before the turn of the century. Colin Kilgarry—who was, apparently, a top-brass detective—dragged Michael Murphy in for the murder of a local fisherman."

"A fisherman? Here? In Cobh?" Connor couldn't help but think of recent events. "Like Keegan?"

"Similar."

"Murphy?" Connor thought for a minute, trying to recall the story—given village gossip, surely he heard of it. "Not many of them in these parts . . ."

"Well, seems it caused enough of a rift to last for decades—information on it stopped, however, after Murphy was found guilty, and townsfolk went on to other things."

"Prison?"

"Life—died only years after his incarceration, screaming he didn't do it as he went to his grave."

"Did he? Do it, I mean . . ."

"Who knows—it was enough for revenge, though. Within a year after Murphy's death, Colin Kilgarry wound up in the same boat as the murder victim."

Connor's eyebrow's arched. "Your kin? Here?"

A nod. "Yes—not far from here."

Connor was quiet, processing what Decklin just told him. "What was the name of the fisherman?"

Momentary silence. "Finnian Kildare."

Wingo inspected her new deckhands' work, a slight smile crossing her lips. She couldn't remember the last time she hired someone remotely competent—at least, according to her expectations. Of the two, she preferred Rowan Murphy to Sean Braniff—but, when she really thought about it, she didn't give a rat's ass about either one of them. As long as they did their jobs, both were fine with her.

Last to leave, as she stepped onto the deserted dock, she turned suddenly, shuddering. "Is someone there," she called.

Silence.

Again, she scanned the docks, hair on the back of her neck beginning to bristle like an alerted dog's hackles. "Hello?" She waited, listening carefully, lightly resting her fingers on her knife's sheath.

Nothing.

Now, it was one thing for Wingo McNamara to feel uncomfortable—it was quite another to feel spooked. Quickly, she headed up the dock, keenly tuned into her surroundings . . .

All the way to Shannon's.

"Well?"

Sean Braniff shrugged. "What can I say? It was my first day—you know no one is going to say anything to the new guy." A pause. "Give me time . . ."

"We don't have time."

Braniff stiffened, then took a long draw from his pint. "I'm afraid you don't have a choice . . .'

Perhaps not the best answer.

Dominic Delgado stood, then leaned over, whispering in Braniff's ear. "It's you who doesn't have a choice . . ."

With that, he headed for the door, then stopped and turned, saying nothing. No need.

The well-launched glare was quite enough.

Chapter 9

From his time as a detective, there was one, basic tenet Decklin Kilgarry knew to be true—when emotions were involved?

Anything was on the table.

So, when he learned of the century old family feud between his ancestors and the Kildare clan, it naturally piqued his interest. But, there was more—also piquing his interest was Finnian Kildare. Coincidence? Maybe.

But, he doubted it.

When first beginning his so-called investigation, it didn't occur to him ulterior motives close to home may come into play. Finn Kildare seemed a trustworthy sort when Decklin first met him, but that wasn't to say skeletons weren't lurking. Of course, they were—and, they were enough to set Detective Decklin Kilgarry on a new path to discovering the truth about Keegan Sullivan's murder.

When names begin to circle, it's time to take notice—something he learned from his mentor when he was a beat cop decades prior. "Although a murder may be random, Kilgarry," his superior told him, "what lies within the murder seldom is . . ."

Words Decklin never forgot.

Laptop comfortable on his lap, he tapped the keys, a search into the lives of village locals top priority. Something was just beneath the surface . . .

Something someone doesn't want him to know.

As expected, Keegan Sullivan's murder morphed from something on people's lips to a forgotten fact of life, leaving little for discussion during passing weeks. Wingo McNamara enjoyed newfound success with both of her new deckhands, bringing in more money than previous years. Convinced she made prudent decisions in hiring them, thoughts of amping up her salmon fishing began permeating her few layers of common sense. Ideas of increasing her one-trawler fleet began to surface, the lure of raking in more money guiding each one. *Surely,* she thought, *if I can achieve this kind of success every year?*

Well, it was almost too much to consider.

Still, she did, attributing her recent luck to Sean Braniff for turning her on to new waters. Of course, they weren't really new, but they were on the fringe of where few wanted to fish. Known for poachers, villagers preferred to stay away, allowing their livelihoods to sink to new lows, refusing to make waves. It was a situation Wingo found intolerable, so, when opportunity presented itself, who was she to spit at it with a jaded eye?

As much as her colleagues wanted to reclaim their waters, all were—in her estimation—pitiful right down to the bottom of their waders. According to her, they were all talk and no show, her father among them. "With more boats," she suggested on more than one occasion, "we can make a mark in Cobh!"

Wingo's idea may have been worth considering, but making a mark wasn't what fueled Aidan McNamara's passion for the sea. No, it was more the feeling of accomplishment for him and his family that tickled his maritime desire. "My father and his father before him paid no attention to money," he bellowed at the pinnacle of their mutual—if not momentary—distaste for each other.

But, she wasn't listening.

So, there she stood, on the deck of her trawler, thinking of ways to up the ante of her suddenly burgeoning salmon fishing business. If things continued on her current path, there may be a little left over—at least enough for creativity when it came to making more money. Although her father would disagree and, as incorrigible as she was, there was an element of merit associated with each hair-brained scheme—that's what Aidan called them. In her mind? That was the reason he was still drying the same old boots he bought years ago by the fireplace each evening.

Never enough money.

"Things are going well, I see!" Connor O'Quinn stood on the dock, a smile crossing his face. "It's nice to see at least one of us making a living!" Of course, the smile was only for striking up conversation—the truth was he knew something wasn't right. Wingo McNamara didn't have the smarts to run one trawler, let alone two. Three. A fleet.

"They are, indeed," she grinned as she motioned him aboard.

Connor stepped onto the trawler, yet keeping his distance—easier to keep a surveilling eye on things. "I only have a minute—but, I just wanted to let you know I'm proud of you." He paused. "I've known you a long time, and you're doing the work of ten men."

A slight blush? Maybe—but Wingo would never admit it. "Well, someone has to do it—and, getting a couple of extra deckhands after poor Keegan bought it was a stroke of luck, that's for sure!"

Crass as always, O'Quinn thought, hating the fact he was on her trawler for nothing else other than getting an eye on her operations.

Her deckhands.

They, however, were nowhere to be seen. "Speaking of deckhands," he commented, scanning the trawler, "where are they? Getting a little late to show up, don't you think?" He laughed, hoping he didn't sound too pushy.

"They'll be here!"

"Well, you're certainly doing something right!" With that, he stepped off the boat with a hearty wave. "A good day to ya . . ."

Nothin' but wasted time, he thought has he headed for his own trawler. Suddenly, he turned, stopping at the sound of voices on the far side of the dock carrying more than the speakers anticipated. "Does she suspect," one asked, his voice more than a whisper.

"Why would she? She's making more money than she has in her life—a few more weeks, and she's ours."

Then, nothing.

Quickly, Connor headed for his boat, words he just heard ringing in his mind. Though he didn't recognize the voices, he was certain they didn't belong to Wingo's deckhands—they passed him as they were showing up for work. *So, who*, he wondered as he boarded.

Before casting off for the day's work, he glanced at Wingo's vessel leaving the harbor, certain she was heading for disaster. *Maybe not today, Wingo . . .*

But, soon.

Although used to inclement weather, there was a bitterness in the Cobh stinging rain, signaling the beginning of the end for salmon fishing season. When summer tipped into early fall, a noticeable urgency tinged the air, advising Dominic Delgado he had little time to make the strides he needed before heading to Nova Scotia to oversee operations. With only a small window for making quotas there, it was always prudent to keep a personal eye on things, especially given stringent, country laws. It was a situation causing considerable consternation among the higher ups, so it fell within Delgado's purview to keep things running smoothly.

Of course, that meant having the right people in the right places turning a blind eye to irregularities that may arise. From a pecuniary perspective, keeping such individuals happy was a herculean task in itself, most demanding increased salaries with each passing season. It was during those times, Delgado felt especially pressured—yet, he knew there wasn't anything he couldn't handle. Still—he preferred leaving Ireland knowing the situation in Cobh was under control. And, at that particular moment?

Far from it.

According to his sources, Wingo McNamara was getting a little too mouthy for Delgado's taste, although he expected such a reaction from newfound wealth. Clearly, she wasn't classy enough to keep her mouth shut about such things and, as one might expect, eyebrows raised every time she sounded off under the influence of drink. But, as predictable as she was, the ancestral fisherman—a moniker on which she insisted—was bringing in a tidy sum for her efforts.

There was, however—along with bonuses rewarding his foresight to recognize weakness when he saw it—a niggling thought. Did he make a mistake? Wingo certainly wasn't above shooting her mouth off about his insistence regarding being a part of her life—advertising he didn't need. Even so, there was no one to take her place—but, that didn't mean he couldn't keep his eyes peeled for someone a little more malleable.

Then, there was word Alannah O'Quinn's cousin was sticking his nose where it didn't belong. Smokey caught wind of that little tidbit while a few of Connor's deckhands were taking a load off after a grueling shift. "There's something about that guy," Smokey informed his boss. "My gut tells me to steer clear . . ."

Strong words coming from someone who wasn't particularly bright, his true worth only illuminated by situations requiring more than conversation. So, that left no one to take care of business in Ireland while Delgado kept the Nova Scotia organization's wheels turning without a squeak. It was, by anyone's standards, something needing to be rectified . . .

Sooner, rather than later.

Chapter 10

Finn Kildare took a sip, then leaned back in his chair, thinking of times passed—you know, when life was easier, and people minded their own damned business. When he thought about it, the good old days weren't so long ago—but, when Cobh's livelihood became the target of those who only fished for the money? Tradition couldn't compete.

Of course, it seemed only a few years since things began to deteriorate. But, as he sipped, watching charred logs burn to mere embers, he knew it wasn't so. It was more than a few years since government issued new laws, many to protect interests such as his.

Then, as he drained his glass, thoughts turned to Decklin Kilgarry—as much he wanted to accept him as he did Alannah and Connor, there was something about him he couldn't quite trust. Then again, distrust wasn't anything new to Finnian Kildare, III . . .

It was a way of life.

From the time he was a 'snotty little brat'—that was what his first grade teacher called him when not in earshot of anyone who may betray her true feelings—formal learning wasn't exactly what Finn had in mind. Incorrigible from the day he was born, it was nothing for teachers to schedule private discussions with his parents to address behavioral issues. "It's nothing serious, I'm sure," Mrs. Barnstable commented during one of their private sessions. "But, I'm sure you'll agree strong-arming schoolmates to get his way isn't what we teach . . ."

Naturally, Finn's parents agreed, promising to talk to him as soon as possible. Unfortunately for Mrs. Barnstable, however, their words meant nothing for Finnian Kildare, II was a firm believer in taking what was needed by whatever means—pearls of wisdom handed down to his son.

The truth was Finnian's parents had other things on their minds, and turning their son into something they'd abhor wasn't on the table. No—hardcore fishing had been in their family for more than a century, leathered hands a testament to hard work.

So, by the time Finnian Kildare, III took his rightful place at the helm of his parent's trawler, education wasn't one of books and math formulas.

It was one of 'get while the gettin' is good.'

Luckily, an education beyond high school wasn't needed for their line of work, and when Finn reached his mid-twenties? Already primed for success. By the time he was thirty-five? Everyone knew his name.

Not necessarily a good thing.

Finn Kildare had a way about him that wasn't good, and why Connor O'Quinn had anything to do with him was a question causing locals to scratch their heads. But, as long as Finn stayed on the right side of Cobh fishing interests, who's business was it to consider his life other than what they knew? As far as they could tell, Kildare was as outraged as anyone when it came to salmon poaching, and he wasn't afraid to tell anyone what he felt. "My family's been in County Cork for generations," he bellowed at Shannon's one rainy night. "I'll never let them win!"

Naturally, there was a round of raucous applause, fisherman filled with one beer too many agreeing by toasting—to them, Finnian Kildare had their best interests at heart.

Or, so they hoped.

Docking in the dark wasn't optimal, but, if it meant a bigger haul, then that's what had to happen. "We're pulling out before dawn," Wingo ordered as Murphy and Braniff finished their duties for the day. "No excuses . . ."

Neither man acknowledged her command as they disembarked, fondness for Wingo McNamara waning with every moment. When agreeing to work for her, neither considered the verbal abuse she could dish out, although both knew of her proclivity to do so.

Moments later, Murphy and Braniff parted ways where the docks turned toward the village, Rowan Murphy cursing the day he agreed to work on McNamara's trawler. Dissatisfaction, however, wasn't quite enough to encourage looking for something else—besides, he wasn't there for the fishing, and his pocketbook proved it.

Checking his watch, he turned toward the Blarney Pub, again cursing Wingo for making him late. "Bitch," he murmured as he finally pulled open the tavern door. Seconds later, he pulled a chair from Finn Kildare's table. "Sorry, mate—couldn't be helped."

Kildare said nothing, gestured to the barkeep, then sat back in his chair. "Wingo?"

"Who else?" Murphy paused, trying not to think about his day as the server placed a pint in front of him. "One of these days, I'm not going to keep my mouth shut . . ."

Finn smiled. "No sense in being hasty, mate. Don't let her get to you—the season's almost over."

"Maybe—but, I'll tell you one thing. Don't expect me to work for her next season . . ."

Kildare bristled. He wasn't used to someone he barely knew dishing directives. "Really? Are you forgetting how much I'm paying you?"

Murphy said nothing, recognizing going against Finn Kildare might not be the smartest move—and, he was right. There was something about the young deckhand Kildare didn't particularly like and, if speaking the truth, he'd admit there was a certain duplicity involved with Murphy's employment. "What do you have for me," he finally asked, figuring it prudent to get on with the reason for their meeting.

"Other than Wingo McNamara is a raving lunatic?"

A nod. "That's a given—you know what I mean." Finn scanned the small tavern to be certain no one was overly interested in his business.

"After we docked, she greeted someone on the trawler—Braniff and I were already to the end of the dock, so I couldn't see who it was."

Kildare was quiet, wondering who Wingo McNamara would be meeting so late at night, especially after a long day of fishing. "Another fisherman?"

Murphy shot him a glare, Kildare's tone getting on his last nerve. "I just said I couldn't see—it was too dark."

"Voices?"

A nod, then a long draw on his pint. "Yep."

Finn tried not to show his mounting exasperation—if Rowan Murphy decided to bolt, he was no closer to exposing the poaching ring than he was at the beginning of the season. "Did you recognize it?"

A slight smirk. "Wingo's."

Kildare was quiet for a moment, deciding how he needed to handle his employee. "A brilliant deduction for one so limited . . ."

"What's that supposed to mean?"

"Only that you can't be that bright if you're copping an attitude with the hand that feeds you." A pause. "Perhaps, you should try again . . ." Sage advice delivered with a convincing glare.

Advice Murphy chose to follow. "Whoever it was," he finally divulged, "McNamara was glad to see him."

"Him?"

"Just a feeling . . ."

"Did you look to see who it was?"

"That's what you're paying for, isn't it?" Murphy guzzled the last of his beer, then stood. "I still couldn't see anyone." A pause. "But, what you might really want to know is why we were fishing in the dark . . ."

Kildare's eyebrows arched. "Enlighten me . . ."

"We were where we shouldn't be, and Braniff was lighting the way." Again, he paused as he lit a cigarette, knowing he had Kildare's attention.

"You mean the other deckhand Wingo hired was advising her where to fish?"

A nod. "Knew the area pretty well, I'd say . . ."

Finn was quiet, weighing what he just heard. "Are you fishing the same area tomorrow," he finally asked, thinking he may need to take a leisurely cruise the following morning.

"Who knows? But, from what we brought in today?" Rowan Murphy grabbed his coat. "A pretty good bet . . ."

Decklin glanced at Alannah, then focused his attention on her husband. "How well do you know Finn Kildare," he asked as he pulled a small notepad from his jacket pocket.

Alannah smiled, then passed a plate of toast to her cousin. "Not well, but he's been around here forever except for a period of time when he was off doing something else. Connor knows him better than I do." She paused before passing the jam. "Don't you, Dear?"

"Well, yes—but, after we talked, Decklin, it occurs to me I know as much about Finn Kildare as he wants me to know."

Alannah glanced at both of them, a slight frown beginning to bloom. "What aren't you telling me?"

"Nothing, really," Decklin answered with a smile. "I'm just trying to figure out who killed Keegan Sullivan."

"Well, what does Finn Kildare have to do with it?"

"Probably nothing—I'm just doing a little research on people who may have known Keegan better than most."

"As far as I know, Finn Kildare and Keegan Sullivan didn't travel in the same circles—and, if they did, it would be because Keegan provided something Finn needed."

"Why do you think that," Connor asked as he accepted the jam from Decklin.

"Because everyone knows Finn Kildare gets what he wants—he's been that way since grade school!"

"You went to school with him," Decklin asked.

"Of course! Both of us have roots here—his family's been here as long as mine!"

In that moment, Decklin and Connor realized it may have been a mistake to not include Alannah in their conversations. "But, you said you don't know him well," her husband commented.

"I don't—Finn Kildare was someone I didn't care for from the time I laid eyes on him in third grade." A pause. "There's just something about him I don't trust . . ."

"But, he was in our house only a few months ago!" Connor couldn't quite believe what he was hearing, wondering why he didn't pick up on his wife's true feelings about their guest.

"Yes, but it wasn't up to me to intrude—besides, you didn't ask."

Decklin listened, their banter not exactly playful. "Okay—it doesn't really matter. What I do need from you, Alannah, is everything you know about Finn Kildare."

"Well, all I can tell you is from the time we were in school together, Finn Kildare was nothing but a bully, and he was always getting in trouble."

"At school?"

A nod. "And, around town when he was in high school." Another pause. "He barely made it through . . ."

"School?"

"Yes—but, he didn't care. He refused to follow rules and, to me, it seemed he always had a chip on his shoulder."

Connor didn't take his eyes from her—everything she was telling them were things he never considered. "Do you know why?"

Alannah shook her head. "No—but he was always fighting with someone, and it seemed to get worse as he got older."

"How?"

"Well, even though Finn was good looking and girls fawned all over him because he was a bad boy, I always felt there was something deeper." She paused, taking a sip of tea. "It seemed to get worse as he got older—he never cared about anything he did, or people he hurt."

Connor's eyes narrowed. "Did he hurt you?"

"Good heavens, no! For all of his charm, I thought he was the most self-centered guy in school!"

Her husband relaxed slightly, still somewhat disturbed by the fact his wife knew Finn Kildare far better than he knew.

"What about his parents," Decklin asked. "Did you know them?"

Again, Alannah shook her head. "Not really—from what I remember, his father didn't have much to do with the family. Whenever I saw Finn outside of school, he was always with his mom. Until high school . . ."

"Then?"

"His father was involved in some sort of legal hassle, but I don't remember what it was . . ." A bite of toast. "But, after his father was hauled in for questioning about whatever it was, Finn wasn't the same."

"In what way?"

"He became more out of control than he already was..."

"Sounds as if his family was pretty dysfunctional..."

Alannah nodded. "That's an understatement!"

Within the hour, Decklin stood, then gave his cousin a quick kiss on her cheek. "Thank you," he commented, as he slipped on his jacket.

"For what? Breakfast?"

"Well, yes—but, thank you for pointing me in the right direction."

"About Finn?"

Without answering, Decklin nodded, shook hands with Connor, then headed for the door, shooting an affectionate smile at his cousin. "I'll be in touch..."

Chapter 11

The following morning, there was little doubt—fall staked its claim, Cobh's fishermen eyeing what little time might be left of their season. If things went their way, three weeks, at best—if not?

Done.

As brittle, stinging rain splatted against the trawler's small window making visibility less than acceptable, Wingo stripped off her fingerless gloves and blew on her hands, hoping to warm them before inspecting the nets. *A devil's day*, she thought as she reviewed her targeted fishing location. If weather conditions persisted, it would be a rough trip to their previous grounds—to her, however?

Nothing was out of bounds.

It was nobody's business what she did, or when she did it—and, she wouldn't hesitate to tell them so. The current issue was dealing with Dominic Delgado—when she signed on to fish waters normally outside of competitors' boundaries, the only thought was about money and how it could catapult her to the head of the pack. Several weeks prior, parking her boots beside Delgado's seemed a good business decision. But, as the season progressed, it became painfully clear he considered himself CEO of her fishing operation—something she would never allow to happen. When she tried asserting her authority?

Slammed.

But, much like her father, it wasn't Wingo's way to accept direction from someone whom she barely knew, so, as she waited for her deckhands to arrive for their shifts, a snippet of revenge began to burrow. After thinking about it carefully, it wasn't that she were dissatisfied—it had more to do with control. She refused to relinquish it, and when someone outside of Cobh tried to usurp her ancestral right? Well, let's just say she didn't cotton to the idea.

The other thing? As much as she would've liked to talk to her father about it, doing so was out of the question, leaving Wingo to decide upon her own manner of handling things. Something unsavory about Delgado was beginning to surface, and it was only after a bit of serious thinking did she recognize what her colleagues abhorred—an interloper was targeting their lives.

And, she was right smack in the middle of it.

"Detective Walsh?" Decklin extended his hand, knowing he was interrupting—something he hated when trying to do his job in D.C.

"Aye—what can I do for ya?" The diminutive detective stood to accept the handshake, then motioned to a chair in front of his desk,

"Well, I'm not really sure, but I may be able to lend a hand in Keegan Sullivan's murder investigation . . ."

Walsh eyed him, not quite sure what to think. It had been a long time since someone outside of the detective unit offered such a thing. "And, why should I listen to you?"

With that, Detective Decklin Kilgarry from Washington D.C. explained his credentials, paying particular attention to his Irish counterpart's reaction.

"What are you doin' in Cobh?"

More explanation.

Walsh was quiet for a moment, thinking. Finally, he extracted a tablet from his desk drawer, then clicked his pen. "Connor and Alannah O'Quinn are good people . . ."

"Indeed, they are—I appreciate their offering to take me in for a month or two." Decklin smiled, knowing he had Walsh's attention. "And, when I heard about Sullivan, I didn't want to intrude."

"Why now?"

Again, Decklin took his time answering—there was no reason to explain suspicions regarding Finn Kildare, so it was prudent to keep the conversation trained only on Sullivan. "Well, although I'm certainly not in the thick of things, it seems as if you may be at a standstill." He paused. "But, as I said, it's not my intent to intrude—I just may be able to bring a little something extra to your investigation." A smile. "After all of my years in the D.C. department, I hope I can do some good!"

Detective Walsh sat back, a glimmer of amusement in his eyes. "Don't we all?" He clicked his pen and leaned forward again, turning to a clean page on the tablet. "Okay. I'm listening . . ."

"Well—as I said, I don't really know much, other than what villagers are saying. And, lately, it hasn't been much, so I'm curious about a few things . . ."

"Such as?"

A pause. "Okay—for starters, all I know about Keegan Sullivan is he liked to tip a few, and he's been around Cobh his whole life . . ."

"Correct."

Although Decklin didn't expect Walsh to be chatty, it was clear he was listening before talking. "Having been here that long, I imagine he had a few people in his life who didn't think highly of him."

"Correct."

Time for direct questions. "Do you think any of them could've had anything to do with it?"

"Detective Kilgarry—Keegan Sullivan was nothing but a drunk who, if he were lucky, kept a job for more than a couple of weeks at a time. As unfortunate as his murder was, the village forgot about it a few weeks after it happened." He subconsciously clicked his pen a few times, but didn't write. "You know—out of sight, out of mind."

"I get it—but, I recall hearing from Connor there were detectives from your Special Unit investigating. As I understand it, they spoke to a few fishermen, then went out on Wingo McNamara's trawler . . ."

"They may have . . ."

From Walsh's answers, it was clear Decklin needed to tread carefully, yet get on with it. "I know you're busy, Detective Walsh, so my point is this . . ."

A nod.

"My gut tells me there's much more to poor Keegan Sullivan's being in the wrong place at the wrong time . . ." A pause. "And, my experience tells me he was offed for a reason—a good reason in the mind of the killer."

Although Detective Graham Walsh was a man who normally kept salient points of an investigation to himself, there was something about Decklin Kilgarry he trusted. "I agree with you . . ."

"Is the case still being investigated?"

Walsh shook his head. "We were ordered to move on."

"By?"

A slight smile. "You know how it is, Detective—when word comes down from on high, we do what we're told."

"Indeed." Silence for a few seconds. "What do you think, Detective? Who do you think killed Keegan Sullivan?"

Walsh gently placed his pen on top of the tablet, signaling notes weren't necessary for what he was about to say. "Are we officially working together?"

Decklin grinned. "I hope so! Between the two of us, I think we can figure it out." He hesitated, though, knowing Walsh would be going against orders. "We can't let it impact you, however . . ."

"I can take care of myself . . ."

Another smile. "Okay—how about if you go first?"

Although Wingo didn't feel like getting into any sort of tiff with her deckhands, she simply couldn't tolerate such lack of respect for punctuality. "You're late, Braniff!"

Her lightly-seasoned deckhand shrugged. "I woke up late . . ."

An honest answer, no doubt, but turning his back on his boss probably wasn't the best choice. Without a thought, Wingo grabbed his jacket sleeve, swinging him around to meet her face-to-face. "Let's get this straight, Braniff—I expect you to be on time, every time." A pause. "And, I can see from the look in your eyes, I'm making myself clear . . ."

Braniff said nothing, surging anger about to get the best of him. Delgado's words from their previous conversation echoed in his brain, tempting Braniff to make good on his promise—but, timing was everything. "It won't happen again. It's just that . . ."

"It's just what?"

He hesitated, adding a nice touch of artistic drama to their conversation. "Nothing . . ."

Watching as Braniff headed for the nets, Smokey monitored the conversation from the bait bucket. Of course, being sixth in command within Delgado's organization, it was up to him to claw his way to the top despite possible concerning consequences—and, ratting out anyone standing in his way seemed a good way to do it. As he crushed his cigarette into the coffee can beside the bait, one thing was certain—if anyone were to threaten his standing with Delgado, the situation would be quickly rectified.

Although not Wingo's usual nature, she said nothing as her deckhands got to work—until she realized Rowan Murphy was nowhere to be seen. "Where's Murphy," she yelled.

Silence.

Saying nothing, she glanced at Braniff and Smokey, noticing a different feel on deck. With as much money as both were making, there was no passion for making more. *And*, she thought, *there's only one reason for that* . . .

Palms were greased by someone else.

Chapter 12

Finn Kildare adjusted the binos as the sound of a trawler's engine cut through rough water, another dank, rainy day compromising his view. Quickly, he wiped raindrops from the lenses, then tried again. *Damn it!* Again, he swiped them with his sleeve, attempting to identify who was on board.

Impossible.

Scanning the horizon for other fishermen, there was no doubt Wingo McNamara was heading toward dangerous waters—something he doubted she'd do of her own volition. For all of her bluster, she wasn't as tough as everyone thought, but few knew it. Even those who knew her from the time she was at the helm of Aidan's trawler had no idea she wasn't who she appeared to be. "You're weak, Wingo McNamara," Kildare muttered to himself as he kept his eyes trained on her vessel. "And, it will be nothing to take you down . . ."

Thanks to Murphy, it was easy to pinpoint where the trawler was headed, but, without cover to disguise his interest, all he could do was keep an eye on her from afar. If he knew Wingo as well as he thought, she wouldn't be paying attention to anything going on around her—an attribute that may serve him well in the future.

So, there he waited, moored under cover of the jagged shoreline of a small island not far from illegal fishing grounds. If anyone were looking, he'd be difficult to spot—and, to those who weren't paying attention.

Invisible.

Detectives Walsh and Kilgarry stood in the driving rain, the Irishman pointing to exactly where Keegan Sullivan was found. "Right there," he said, pointing. "Under the dock . . ."

Kilgarry scanned the entire area, then focused on the shallow shoreline water. "How long until someone found him?"

"Hours—the coroner pinpointed he was dead between twelve and two."

"A.M., I presume?"

A nod.

"What did he find?" Decklin glanced at Detective Walsh, again scanning nearby docks. "Drowning?"

"Not exactly . . ."

"Dead before he was dumped?"

"Dumped? Why do you say that?" Graham eyed him, wondering if Decklin heard information from someone else—and, if that were the case, the question was who told him.

"Because from what I saw at the town meeting, Keegan Sullivan was a brawny man—taking him out where there may be prying eyes could cause quite a ruckus."

"I thought of that . . ."

"Did you check it out?"

Detective Walsh shook his head. "Didn't have to—the investigation was pulled before I had a chance."

"Do you know why?"

Walsh focused on Detective Kilgarry, knowing what he was about to tell him could get him canned should anyone learn of their conversation. "After the Special Unit guys wrapped up their gone-in-sixty-seconds investigation, I was told to never speak of it again . . ." A brief pause. "I was told to let it lie."

Having been in a similar situation early in his career, Decklin was well aware of pitfalls when it came to police puppeteers. "I get it—your office was where truth goes to die."

"In a manner of speaking . . ."

Decklin glanced at him, recognizing reticent resignation. "Did they threaten you?"

"You mean a 'men in black' sort of thing?" Another pause. "It was veiled . . ."

"Usually is."

With rain beginning to morph into something more unpleasant, conversation was the last thing on their minds as they headed back to Detective Walsh's office, neither perceiving a figure in a dark rain slicker following from a distance. Even so, Decklin turned, again scanning the docks and village shoreline. "Did you hear something?"

Walsh looked at him, grinning. "In this weather? We'd be lucky to hear a trawler pulling into dock!"

Still, Detective Kilgarry stood still, his head bowed slightly as he listened intently. "You're right," he finally acquiesced.

Walsh stopped, focusing his attention on the only man who had the guts to take on Keegan Sullivan's murder. "You'll hear a lot of things around these docks, Kilgarry . . ." He paused, thinking about their intended trajectory toward solving the killing. "Most of it not good . . ."

"Docks are rarely a pleasant place to be . . ."

By the time they reached the small, Cobh station house, neither felt like talking, both eager to get warm. "You realize," Walsh commented as they parted, "we're opening a can of worms . . ."

Nothing more than a nod.

Still moored out of sight, Finn Kildare kept an eye on the Lavender Shamrock—the trawler Wingo named when she was a child, much to the chagrin of her father—until it headed back to port. As much as he hated navigating in the dark, there was little choice as he followed, waiting far enough off shore before docking to deflect suspicion. Hating to admit he returned with nothing to show for his time, it was clear he had a decision to make as he headed for Shannon's once his boots stepped onto dry land.

As darkness offered its cloak, he finally sat at a table in Shannon's recesses, ordered a healthy portion of fish and chips, then waited for Wingo and her crew to make an appearance. *She'll be here*, he thought as he took the first sip of a stout pint.

He was right.

Within twenty, Wingo McNamara yanked open the tavern door, deckhands obviously not in tow—something Kildare thought odd after a long, cold day on the water. But, what really caught his eye?

Dominic Delgado.

He watched as Delgado gestured discreetly to catch Wingo's attention, smiling as she took a seat in case anyone were looking. Not long after, both appeared to be enjoying an evening meal together, chatting as if they were old friends.

Kildare, however, knew better and, as he contemplated the topic of their conversation, his cell vibrated. Quickly, he checked his message, downed the rest of his pint, then headed for the door, all the while keeping an eye on Delgado and his dinner guest.

Something's up, he thought as he stepped outside into relentless rain—unfortunately, though, he didn't have time to give the unlikely supper mates a second thought.

Rowan Murphy wasn't the patient type.

"The numbers are good," Delgado commented as he buttered a biscuit, then crammed it in his mouth.

Wingo grinned and sat back, draining the last of her beer. "Never been better!" She hesitated, briefly wondering if she should spill the beans about buying another trawler—but, since she wasn't exactly the contemplative type, the thought lasted less than a second or two. "In fact," she continued, "I'm thinking of picking up another vessel..."

Dominic buttered another biscuit. "Do you think that's a good idea?"

"Why wouldn't it be? Everything's going fine—you're taking your cut, and I'm still making more money than I have in years!"

"That's true—but, what about hiring the deckhands, and someone to captain it? That costs money..."

"Yes, but, with what I have going on now, I don't think

either will be a problem . . ." Although she realized Delgado was most likely thinking about how much he could make from such a move, she didn't really care. After all, she had no intention of his horning in on her success for another year—why would she? She had everything she needed, and then some—the way she saw it, Dominic Delgado helped her out of a jam, and that was the end of it.

Ignorance?

Of course. Or, stupidity . . .

Delgado wasn't quite sure.

"Braniff and Smokey are planning something . . ." Rowan Murphy took a drag from his cigarette, then blew three impressive smoke rings before focusing on Finn. "Seems those two are a little cozier than we thought . . ."

"Where was Wingo?"

"In the wheelhouse stuffing her face, as usual . . ."

"Okay . . ." Finn's cue for Murphy to continue.

"It seems they're planning a move against their bitch of a captain."

"Mutiny?"

Murphy laughed, then took another drag. "With three?" Again, he laughed, causing people to look. "Hardly what I call a mutiny, mate . . ."

"Call it what you will—what did they say?"

"Well, I couldn't hear clearly, mind ya, but it sounds as if they have plans . . ."

"Plans to do what?"

Murphy crushed his cigarette in the tavern's dirty ashtray. "What do you think?" A pause. "Offing her."

Finn stared at him, stunned. "Are you bloody serious?"

A smile. "Never been more . . ."

And, so it begins, Kildare thought as he considered the weight of what Murphy just divulged. "Do they have any idea you heard them?"

"I'm not that stupid. Had me earplugs in—just no music."

Within a few minutes, Rowan Murphy stood, then threw enough on the table to cover the cost for both of them. "This one's on me." With that, he was gone, leaving Finn with a mighty dilemma . . .

Open his mouth, or keep his yap shut?

There was, however, one more thing worth considering— rumor had it Alannah O'Quinn's cousin was snooping. If Braniff and Smokey made good on their idea? *Guess who would be first on the scene* . . . A thought he chose not to entertain—at least for the time being. *A Kilgarry in my midst?*

How lucky can one man get?

"The fire feels good tonight, doesn't it?" Alannah smiled at her cousin and husband, then bid her usual early goodnight to both. "I'll leave you to it, then . . ."

"Thanks, again," Decklin called to her as she headed upstairs, then turned his focus to Connor. "She's one hell of a cook!"

"Indeed, she is!" Connor patted his stomach. "I keep saying she's the reason I need to watch my waistline!"

Then, a quiet few moments as both men considered topics for discussion. "How about you go first," Connor suggested as he took a sip of his Irish coffee.

Following suit, Decklin nodded. "It was an interesting day," he began. "I decided to drop in on Detective Graham Walsh . . ."

"Unannounced, I take it . . ."

A nod. "Doing so usually yields better results."

"This time?"

"Same." Again, both men were silent until Decklin continued. "A hard man to read," he finally commented, "but, we're working together on Sullivan's murder."

"Together?"

"So it seems—although it might not have been the best decision. Bringing me into the mix puts him in a precarious position . . ."

"That may be—but, knowing Graham Walsh as I do, he prefers to ferret out the truth rather than protect his own skin."

"Exactly the impression I got when he took me to the precise place where Keegan's body was found . . ."

Connor took a sip of his coffee, eyebrows arching. "Is the case still open?"

Decklin shook his head. "Nope—it came down from the top he was to put the investigation to bed."

"Did he say that?"

A nod. "He also said he was threatened by Special Unit guys to drop it . . ."

"Not surprising—so, that was that."

Decklin was quiet, thinking about the danger he and Walsh could be in if anyone caught wind of Kilgarry's involvement. No matter his last name, villagers wouldn't take well to a foreigner meddling in their affairs, even if it regarded solving the murder of one of their own. "Not quite— we agreed to work independently, funneling information to each other without anyone's noticing. If we can do that, there's a good chance we can bring to justice whomever decided Keegan Sullivan was about to live his last day on earth." A pause. "That's all I want . . ."

Connor eyed him, a slight smile on his lips. "It'll be harder than you think—folks around here are pretty tight-lipped. Talking to strangers doesn't interest them . . ."

"A stranger? I've been here three months! I should be a local by now!"

"Fat chance . . ."

Chapter 13

Within the month, weather turned as the salmon season closed unceremoniously, some fishermen happy with their achievements, others lamenting the fact they'd need to find another line of work.

Bolstered by newfound success, Wingo's decision to increase her bounty with a second trawler wasn't exactly met with energetic enthusiasm among her peers, leaving most who knew her well to wonder if she lost her marbles. But, it was their next thought making everyone realize doing something so reckless during difficult times wouldn't endear her to her colleagues. "She's throwing it in our faces," more than one villager lamented during private conversations.

Most agreed.

Of course, such sentiments were understandable—a good chunk of Cobh's fishing business was disappearing at an alarming rate due to illegal poaching, and there wasn't a damned thing anyone could do about it. Or, if there were, no one bothered to take the initiative, bitter complaining seeming much more to their liking—either way, there was no question something needed to be done.

"If my colleagues can't get it together enough," Wingo commented to one of her two friends at the close of the season, "that's not my fault!" An interesting interpretation of her village's problems to be sure, likely diminishing her popularity factor to zero.

So, as one might imagine, it came as no surprise when her water-logged body was spotted bobbing against a large boulder just north of the village with no visible signs of foul play—at least with binos. "She was probably lit," her father commented when Graham Marsh delivered the news. Then, Aidan thanked the detective, politely dismissing him so his family could grieve in private.

As with any small village, within twenty-four word circulated, some not disguising the fact they hated Wingo McNamara's guts, and she got exactly what she deserved. Others—Decklin Kilgarry and Graham Walsh among them—realized something greater was afoot, and it was time to begin ferreting out the reason for the stain on their beloved village. What they really wanted?

Another town hall.

A few months prior, it might've been a good idea, but with two murders on their hands, the last thing Detective

Walsh needed was townsfolk getting their hands dirty in his business. "We need to change our trajectory," Decklin commented when they met before Wingo's wake. "You and I know this is far beyond coincidence . . ."

Graham nodded as he watched mourner's file into the small chapel west of the village. "Whoever did this will be here . . ."

"Do you see anyone who doesn't belong?" Decklin paused, also eyeing those who were making their way to small pews just behind Aidan and his wife.

"Not yet—but, as you can see, there's more curiosity going on rather than mourning McNamara's unfortunate passing." Inconspicuously, he gestured toward a group of women who seemed far too exuberant considering the circumstances.

"Well, from what I hear, Wingo wasn't the best liked person in town . . ."

"That's putting it mildly—when she started flashing money around Shannon's, talking about buying another trawler, there wasn't a fisherman in town who wanted to listen."

Both men were quiet as the funeral service began, each taking mental notes of what didn't seem quite right. Number one on both of their lists?

Hardly anyone showed up.

Number two?

Braniff and Murphy.

No shows.

Dominic Delgado lit a cigarette, then focused on the man sitting across from him. "Our season was better than we anticipated," he commented. "Enough to make up for deficiencies elsewhere . . ."

Carmine Ingancius Borja kept his attention on the papers in front of him, interested in only one thing. "It has come to my attention," he finally stated, "there are two mysterious deaths in Ireland."

"That's . . ."

"Imbécil!" With a deft hand, Borja pulled a handkerchief from his pocket, then removed his glasses, swiping at the lenses with irritated strokes. Moments later, specs again in place, he lit a cigar and sat back in his chair, never taking his eyes from the man who came to him so highly recommended. In his mind?

Not cuttin' it.

Dominic said nothing the more pissed he became. He always regarded Carmine Borja a self-aggrandizing, ignorant ass, and it was clear by his comment he had no idea how to handle certain situations when they presented themselves. Finally, he mustered a small semblance of restraint. "Cobh is small . . ."

A glare. "Was it you?"

"Me," Delgado asked, genuinely surprised by what he considered a stupid question. "Why would I take money from both of us by doing such a thing?" He paused, knowing he was over his target.

"Surely," Borja countered, "you are aware of my feelings about deceit . . ."

"Indeed—I assure you, I had nothing to do with either."

Borja tilted his head back and closed his eyes, swirling ice cubes in the cocktail glass he held on his lap. "Tell me what you know . . ."

Delgado took a final drag on his cigarette, then placed it in the ashtray in front of him, smoke continuing to waft slightly. "Like I said, I didn't have anything to do with it . . ."

"Both were in your employ, were they not?"

"Well, yes . . ."

"Then it was your responsibility to look after their best interests."

"I hardly think . . ."

Borja opened his eyes, then took a sip. "I know—I've always contended it's your greatest deficiency." Launching another glare, he couldn't help thinking he'd been a bit hasty when hiring Delgado five years prior. It wasn't that he was slow to catch on to Borja's requirements for executing the job—it was something far worse. After such a spate of time, it was becoming increasingly clear Dominc Delgado didn't have the killer instinct.

A deep breath as Delgado ignored the sleight. "As I was saying, I had nothing to do with either—so, someone else must be decreasing the population."

"And, just who would that be?"

Dominic shook his head. "I don't know . . ."

A pause and sip. "Then, it is up to you to find out—you will return, and conduct an investigation." Another pause. "An investigation for me . . ."

As much as he hated bringing locals into his investigations, Graham Walsh knew and understood the importance of privacy. "Thank you for inviting me into your home," he commented as Alannah greeted him at the door, holding her hand out as a signal to peel his slicker and hand it to her.

"You're more than welcome!" Shaking his jacket before hanging it up, she pointed to the sitting room. "They're in there—I'll bring in dessert and coffee, then leave you to discuss important things!" She smiled, shooed him toward her husband and cousin, then disappeared.

"Gentlemen!" Walsh grinned, shook hands with each, then directed his attention to Connor. "Alannah gets prettier every day—how she wound up with a coot like you, I have no idea!" Then, he acknowledged Decklin, taking a seat across from him. "We have much to discuss . . ."

Decklin nodded. "Indeed we do . . ."

"My wife and I haven't been out and about since . . ." Connor glanced at both men. "You know . . ." Even though Wingo McNamara wasn't one of his favorite people, he firmly felt it was appropriate to show a modicum of respect.

"Wingo?"

"Aye—and, there's no doubt in my mind the person who killed poor Keegan is one and the same."

Graham said nothing, paying close attention to Connor as he spoke. Of all people in their village, he always impressed Detective Walsh as a straight shooter.

"Five years ago, this wouldn't have happened," Connor continued. "Nobody woulda thought such a thing . . ."

"Then," Decklin interrupted, "it seems we need to start with what changed five years ago." He turned to Graham. "Do you agree?"

Just as Detective Walsh was about to answer, Alannah appeared with apple tarts and Irish coffees arranged beautifully on an antique tray. "Get 'em while they're hot," she suggested before excusing herself for the evening.

"Wait . . ."

She turned, surprised at the urgency in her cousin's voice. "Did I forget something?"

Decklin grinned, then glanced at Connor and Graham. "Why don't you stay?" Again, he focused on the men. "I'm pretty sure Alannah will beef up our investigation . . ."

Connor's wife blushed, then sat beside him on the small love seat. "Well, my . . . I don't know what I can add!"

From there?

Off and running.

Chapter 14

*S*ince the time Dominic Delgado was a kid running the streets in coastal Spain, rules didn't apply. Ever. So, when Carmine Borja ordered him back to Ireland, it was something he didn't take lightly. The only plus was lodging wouldn't be an issue. The negative?

He was paying for it out of his own pocket.

Stingy bastard, he thought, the sea appearing on his right as he drove into the village's sunset. *He'll pay* . . . But, there were things to do before assuaging a niggling, growing vengeance—things like finding out what the hell happened to Braniff after he paid him for the season. "He's nothing but a punk," he muttered, turning left, then right, to an out-of-the-way boarding house he discovered during the last salmon season.

Settled within the hour, after a shower and a bite to eat, Delgado turned his attention to his most urgent matters, confident no one would be coughing up information any time soon. Knowing that, it behooved him to locate Braniff to, once more, be his eyes and ears—if that didn't work? *I'll think of something,* he thought as he searched the Internet for information about Sullivan's and Wingo's murder.

Too bad there was little to find.

A purposeful media omission? Probably. But, he had to admit there was little to write about other than the fact both were found in water, both were drunks and loudmouths, and no one really cared what happened to either. *At least, that's what they should've said . . .*

What the village writers really said?

Both would be missed.

Fat chance . . .

"So, what do you think?"

Alannah frowned, slightly uncomfortable discussing the village murders with her husband and cousin, as well as the town's chief detective. "Well, I'm not sure . . ."

Decklin smiled, sensing her reluctance. "Alannah, you know the people in this village better than anyone—so, let's start with how things were five years ago. Before the poaching issue blew in . . ."

"Oh, it was nothing like it is now! Back then—even though it wasn't long ago—people enjoyed each other, and it was nothing to stop on a corner to engage in a little town gossip!"

"Now?"

She eyed him, then subconsciously began twirling the end of her hair with her fingertips. "Well, Decklin, you know—when you first got here, people were buttoned up when it came to accepting you."

"I think they still are . . ."

"That's what I mean! Everybody keeps to themselves, and I can only wonder what they talk about when everyone is in for the night. Angry pillow talk, I imagine."

"She's right," Connor agreed. "It seems as if people are afraid of something . . ."

Graham listened, interested in perceptions of people he barely knew and seldom saw. "That's when the poaching crisis came to a head . . ."

Decklin glanced at him. "Five years ago?"

"Yep—ever since then, we started losing townsfolk. Some just packed up and left . . ."

"Any idea as to why?"

Detective Walsh shook his head. "Not really—and, it wasn't any of my business. Alannah's right—back then, life in the village wasn't like it is today and, if anyone were getting out of line, I'd hear about it. If not?" A pause. "Well, let's just say I don't go looking for trouble . . ."

"Now?"

"It finds me..."

Decklin was quiet for a moment, thinking. "So," he finally asked, "who came to town five years ago? Who was new?"

Walsh took his time, mentally cycling through who drifted in and out. "Let me think—I rarely know the names of people who come and go unless they break the law. But, one who comes to mind is a guy named Delgado. I only met him once, but I heard he was knowledgeable about fishing—and, if I'm not mistaken, he worked on a couple of the trawlers." By habit, he pulled a small notepad from his pocket, ready to write down anything remotely interesting. "There was something about him, though..."

"Like what—and, do you recall on whose boat?"

"On whose boat, I'm not sure—maybe Wingo's." A pause. "It wasn't anything specific—more of a feeling, really. But, I do remember hearing a tart from one of our backroom bars thought he walked on water."

"Connor grinned. "I think I know the one—Miranda, if I recall correctly."

Alannah shot him a playful glance. "How would you know?"

"Merely gossip, my dear. Merely gossip..."

"As far as I know," Detective Walsh continued, "he never got himself in hot water with us. I'd know..."

So, the evening progressed, Alannah recounting what she knew about the few new villagers, no one really catching her attention. "Deckhands come and go," she commented when she couldn't recall anyone else, "so, I'm not counting them. I do remember hearing about Delgado, though, from

Heather . . ." She glanced at her husband. "You know—Timothy's wife. From down the road . . ."

"Wouldn't one of the deckhands be a perfect suspect?" Connor glanced at his wife, then focused on Kilgarry and Walsh. "I mean, it's kind of an 'in and out' thing—and, after a long season, most of them leave until the following season. If there is one . . ."

"Are you saying you believe the salmon poaching is directly related to the murders?"

"Why wouldn't it be?" Connor looked to Decklin for confirmation. "It makes sense, doesn't it?"

Decklin took a sip of his Irish coffee as he was thinking. "I think you raise a good point—it's possible and, perhaps, likely."

All eyes turned to Detective Walsh. "What do you think," Decklin asked, not wanting to intrude on Graham's territory.

"Well, if nothing else, it's a damned good place to start—tomorrow, I'll run a check on Delgado." He paused, scribbled a few notes on his notepad, then slipped it back in his pocket. "First name?"

"I don't remember . . ." Alannah focused on the floor for a few seconds, trying to recall the few conversations she had about him with her friend down the road. "But, I'm not really sure—it was a few years ago."

"No matter—it won't take me long to find out what I need." Walsh stood, then extended his hand to Decklin and Connor. "I'll be in touch . . ." Then, he grinned at Alannah. "And, thank you, ma'am! Those apple tarts were just like my mum used to make!"

Minutes later, life returned to normal for the O'Quinns—with one, small exception . . .

Without doubt, a killer lurked in their village.

"You didn't tell me you were in town . . ."

"I wasn't aware I had to . . ." Dominic Delgado looked her up and down, only one thing on his mind. "Not glad to see me?" He reached in his pocket, withdrew a wad, then threw it on the bed.

Quickly, she eyed it, then returned her attention to him. "Of course, I'm glad—it's just a . . . surprise, that's all." Miranda Byrne smiled, a tug of foreboding curdling her stomach. "What brings you back before the next season?"

"Work."

"How long," she asked, snatching the roll of bills, slipping it into a safe place. "And, to answer your question, of course I'm glad to see you . . ."

That was it. Next?

Down to business.

As much as Decklin would've enjoyed a good night's sleep, it simply wasn't to be—too much Delgado on his mind.

The first thing he needed to ascertain was whether Delgado knew Keegan Sullivan and Wingo McNamara—if there were a link between the two, at least he'd have a place to start. Second on his list of things to do?

Finn Kildare.

After learning of his dubious ancestral past, he couldn't dismiss the relentless thought there was something about him Decklin didn't like. *Maybe,* he considered, *I'm tainting the present with the past . . .*

Figuring sleep wasn't in the cards, he slipped into his sweats and slippers, then brewed a cup of tea. Then?

A long night.

By daybreak, Detective Decklin Kilgarry knew two things—one, his gut was pointing him in the right direction regarding Finn Kildare. A night of preliminary, extensive Internet research revealed an activist background, mainly outside of his home village. Whether such political leanings had anything to do with the murders, he didn't know—but, it surely was worth checking out. Recalling his conversation with Alannah weeks prior, she was quite clear about the only reason Kildare would have anything to do with Keegan Sullivan were if he had something Finn needed. "They didn't travel in the same circles," she said, her words burying themselves into Decklin's brain.

So, that was something.

Second?

Delgado.

The more Decklin thought about it, the more he felt there was more to Delgado's potential involvement. There was, however, a slight, unsettling hitch—zero information about anyone named Delgado with a background congruent with his investigation. Of course, there were a few Delgados popping up as he searched, but none provided what he needed.

Knowing those two things, Decklin stashed his legal tablet filled with notes in a desk drawer, then locked it. *No sense in taking chances,* he thought as he headed for a hot shower. *Whoever is picking off fishermen, won't hesitate at taking a swipe at me once word gets out . . .*

"Dominic Delgado . . ." Detective Walsh handed Decklin a manila file folder containing all records he could find pertaining to the Spaniard. "Not much to go on . . ."

Quickly, Decklin leafed through the few pages, not surprised Dominic Delgado kept a low profile. If, in fact, he were involved with salmon poaching in Ireland, it was a good bet he wasn't the mastermind of such an operation—a peon, at best. At least, that's the way he'd be viewed from the hierarchy who was lining his pockets.

It was also a good bet the person calling the shots didn't live in Cobh or anywhere in Ireland—the farther away, the better. "Do we have anything to go on other than this?" Decklin handed Walsh the file, watching as he slipped it into his worn briefcase.

"So far, that's it . . ."

"The paperwork shows he's from Spain—isn't that where the group of poachers caught last season were from?"

Walsh was quiet, the light bulb beginning to blink. "You're right," he finally answered. "Maybe we're on the right track . . ."

"Can you think of anyone else of Spanish descent who's currently in Cobh?"

"No."

Decklin smiled, appreciating the Irish detective's direct answer—no parsing words or embellishment. "Then, why else would he be here?"

"Who knows—you and I know it could be perfectly innocent. And, if I don't have reason to get to know him on a professional basis—if you know what I mean—he'll be free to carry on business."

"Agreed." Then, a change of thought. "Did you notice anyone following you?"

"To here?" Walsh eyed his counterpart, not liking what Decklin was obviously thinking.

A nod.

"No—why?"

"I'm not really sure—but, I get the feeling someone is paying a little too much attention to what I'm doing."

"You think you're being surveilled?"

Another nod. "I'm not sure, but let's put it this way—I wouldn't be surprised."

"I don't like the sound of that . . ."

"Nor do I—but, I also had the same feeling a few months ago. I felt as if someone were watching . . ."

Detective Walsh scanned the room, a disquieting discomfort slowly beginning to rise. "I don't suppose there are cameras . . ."

"Here? I don't think so. . ." A pause. "But, it's not a bad idea—I'll see what I can arrange on the QT." With that, Decklin stood, heading for the door. "For the time being, we need to communicate differently—I'll be in touch."

"Good plan."

As Decklin watched Walsh walk to his car, a familiar feeling took him back to D.C., and his last case. *Someone has an agenda,* he thought. *Something ain't right . . .*

Not right, at all.

Chapter 15

*I*t's always tricky business when something grows roots based on a lie—most times, there's little chance of coming out of such a nasty situation completely unscathed. If there is?

Something worse awaits down the line.

Unfortunately, that piece of sage advice held no particular allure for Dominic Delgado—so, when Sean Braniff once again sat across from him at Shannon's, he had everything worked out.

Always careful to cover his trail during the course of any business opportunity, he knew it would be nothing to pin anything and everything on the young, smart-mouthed deckhand. "So, I'm guessing you're wondering exactly why I summoned you . . ."

"Summoned?" Disdain crossed the deckhand's face, distaste obvious. "I don't do 'summoned' . . ."

"I disagree. You're here, aren't you?"

Always good to set conversational tone with a smidge of authority.

Suddenly, Braniff stood, grabbing his coat from the adjacent chair. "Not anymore . . ."

Delgado smiled, watching as the young hothead strode toward the door, struggling to get his coat on as he crammed a pack of cigarettes into his coat pocket. *You pathetic fool*, he thought, knowing they'd meet again.

He, too, snatched his coat from a chair and headed for the door, stepping into a frigid, Irish night. Scanning the area, a familiar, sudden shudder snaked its way through his body causing him to step back into Shannon's shadows.

Someone had him in the crosshairs.

Decklin thanked the delivery person, eager to send him on his way, then closed and locked the cottage's front door. *Overnight means overnight*, he smiled to himself as he slit the packing tape with his pocket knife. Gently, he lifted four surveillance cameras from the box, assessing each carefully.

Perfect! Then, for the remainder of the afternoon, he set each camera in a strategic location, making certain the perimeter of the cottage was completely within range and connecting with his laptop.

A little excessive? Maybe. *But,* he thought as he fired up his computer to test his handiwork, *it beats being dead . . .*

The hair on the back of his neck beginning to bristle and rise, Delgado again stepped into the glow of Shannon's lamplight, acknowledging the nearby threat. Scanning the street before heading to the boarding house, he stood still, listening for the muffled rustle of brittle winter grass, or movement meant to remain undetected. Then, swiftly, he turned, catching a momentary glimpse of boots rounding the corner. *Wellies,* he thought as he stepped into high gear, hoping to confront whomever it was. Within seconds, he, too, rounded the corner, certain he could catch a glimpse.

Nothing.

Again, he stood, listening.

Finally, jamming his hands in his coat pocket, he returned to the street, certain of one thing . . .

Awareness heightened.

Nearly a month passed with little to show for Decklin's and Walsh's investigative efforts. After Wingo McNamara's funeral and burial, village life returned to normal without much thought given to the village fisherman. You know . . .

Other things to do.

Besides, it was winter and, although Cobh appeared modern and bustling, its core was one of tradition—buttoning up during the months when they couldn't fish.

Alannah O'Quinn, however, wouldn't let anything get in the way of her normal routine. "I'm going to the market," she called to her husband. "Text me if you need anything!" With that, she was gone, leaving her husband to an hour by himself, assured he had plenty to keep him busy.

Heading to the nearest shopping center, she couldn't help but notice the change in her village. It no longer held the charm she adored as a child and, for the first time, she entertained the thought of living somewhere else—only to dismiss it seconds later. Still, there was little doubt history was disappearing, her heart aching with stark realization.

Within twenty, she stood among baskets of produce, mentally placing dinner ingredients in a cast iron pot, all perfect for dissolving the sharpness of a frigid day. As she reached for the potatoes, a hand brushed hers, obviously targeting the same thing, a voice following. "I'm sorry!"

"Nothing to be sorry about," she replied as she turned toward a handsome man—one whom she thought she recognized, but couldn't be sure. Then, a smile. "You go first," she suggested.

"I wouldn't dream of it!" He stepped back, offering her plenty of room.

Another smile. "Thank you . . ."

Well, it wasn't until she was home and unloading the groceries did she recognize who stood beside her at the potato bin. *Good Lord—it had to be him!* Quickly, she grabbed the groceries and hurried inside. "Connor!" No response. "Conner! I'm in the kitchen!"

It wasn't often his wife raised her voice, but, when she did? Important stuff.

"Aye! I'm here! What . . ."

"I saw him! Talked to him!" With fire and excitement in her eyes, she pulled out two chairs, motioning to him. "Sit!"

With a laugh, he joined her at the table. "Okay—who did you see?"

Alannah sat back in her chair. "Delgado."

"What? He's here?"

"I'm certain it was him," she explained, excitement still flashing in her eyes. "He had an accent, and I didn't even think about it until I was on the way home!" She paused, recalling the few moments she had with Decklin's and Walsh's main target. "But, I'm sure it was Dominic Delgado!"

Without comment, Connor reached for his cell phone on the counter, then tapped the screen.

Connected.

"I hope you don't have plans for dinner," he laughed when Decklin answered. Moments later he rang off, then turned to his wife. "There'll be one more . . ."

"That was a great stew," Decklin praised his cousin as she pulled his plate from the table.

"Thank you!" With a good-natured curtsy, she took her husband's plate. "So, what do you think? He's definitely here!"

"I believe you," Decklin assured her. "But, I'm curious as to why Delgado's here in the dead of winter . . ."

"Indeed—that's the question, isn't it? Perhaps for signing on new deckhands before anyone else has the chance—I wouldn't put it past anyone these days to pull such a stunt." Connor watched as his wife placed the dishes in the sink, then return with a teapot kept warm with her grandmother's hand-knitted cozy. "If that's the case, we're in trouble . . ."

"Don't most deckhands stay with the trawler they were on the year before?"

"You'd think so—but, when it comes to money?" Connor paused, thinking of past fishing seasons. "They can easily be bought . . ."

"He's right," Alannah interrupted. "I seldom see the same faces when I'm on our boat." She paused, a contemplative expression crossing her face. "It's kind of sad when I think about it . . ."

Connor nodded. "Aye—but, nothing's going to change until we nail the bastards who're stripping us of our livelihoods!"

"I know—you're right. It's no time for sentiment . . ."

Instantly, regretting his comment, Connor took her hand, giving it a gentle squeeze. "I didn't mean . . ."

With a sudden smile, she gave him a peck on his cheek. "I know!"

A potentially explosive moment behind them, Decklin put another question on the table. "Do we think he's working alone? Delgado, I mean . . ."

Connor shook his head. "I doubt it—if he's involved, it makes sense he'd have someone ferrying information from the trawler's captain."

"Like Wingo? Do you recall who was working her boat?"

"Well, let me think . . ." He tilted his head back, eyes closed. "It wasn't too much before the end of the season," he finally commented, "when I stopped by Wingo's trawler."

"Why?"

Connor opened his eyes, then focused on Decklin. "Snooping. Good old curiosity—I heard she was doing pretty well, and I wanted to know why."

Alannah nodded. "When you think about it, though, it doesn't make much sense. Wingo McNamara wasn't exactly the model captain, and it was more than one deckhand who hated her guts. That's why she never had the same crew for more than a season or two . . ."

Decklin was quiet as he considered the hierarchy of Delgado's organization—if, indeed, he had one. Experience told him Dominic wasn't the top dog, and there had to be someone pulling the strings—someone with deep pockets and a penchant for steamrolling over anyone who stood in the way of the almighty dollar.

"He's not . . ." Suddenly, Decklin sat up a little straighter, his attention on the window at the far end of the kitchen. "Did you see that?"

Connor, too, sat up, looking in the same direction. "See what?"

Knowing not to make himself a target by standing, he gestured to Connor and Alannah to remain seated. Closest to the light switch, he flipped it off, then stood silently, eyes trained on the window.

Nothing.

"What did you see," Alannah asked, exhaling as if she'd been holding her breath the entire time.

"I'm not sure—but, I could've sworn I saw a figure pass by the window."

"All the way out here?" Connor paused, trying to make sense of it. "But, why?"

"That's what I'd like to know—have you ever had trouble with trespassers before?"

"Trespassers? Good heavens, no!" Alannah looked at her husband, alarm beginning to register in her eyes. "Connor! I don't like this!"

Connor squeezed his wife's hand. "Nor do I . . ."

Chapter 16

By the time Decklin made it to his cottage, there was little doubt someone was keeping track of where he went and who he saw—although, to be fair, his whereabouts wouldn't have been too difficult to figure out. Even so, he was on high alert as he walked home, new snow blanketing the country road. *If only this started while I was at Connor's*, he thought, knowing tracks would've been apparent. But, as it was, when he inspected the area at the O'Quinn's, nothing pointed to an intruder.

Still unable to get the evening's conversation out of his mind, he paused at his screened-in porch, scanning the area before approaching the door. If someone did have eyes on him, he would surely feel them—one of his talents catapulting him up the D.C. detective ranks quicker than anyone anticipated.

Suddenly, he stopped as he approached the porch, aware of a different energy.

Nothing.

Then, casually, he walked up the steps, opened the screen door and, once safely inside, flipped the latch.

Switching off the hall lamp he normally kept on during the night, Decklin grabbed his laptop, then headed for the bedroom, away from prying eyes. Pulling the curtain closed, he logged on, finally clicking on the most recent camera footage.

The first hour yielded nothing, prompting Decklin to think he was wrong—until a shadowy figure briefly came into view on the right side of his cottage's perimeter. *I knew it! Yes!* But, as he silently congratulated himself, as suddenly as the hooded figure appeared, it was gone, leaving him no closer to figuring out who was interested. *Someone,* he thought, *knows I'm investigating . . .*

Sean Braniff didn't bother to remove his coat as he sat down across from Delgado. "I told you—I'm not interested."

Delgado said nothing, knowing if he pushed the young deckhand too far, his job would be that much more difficult. The truth was Braniff made good on his tavern promise when he turned his back on the man who could make his life a whole lot easier—yet, backing away from his word wasn't the Braniff way.

A generational thing.

Finally, Delgado spoke. "I suggest we put our differences to the side, and focus on what's important."

"Which is?"

"Finding out who murdered Wingo McNamara . . ."

Braniff snickered, then took a pack of cigarettes from his coat pocket. Extracting the last one, he lit it, then placed it in the ashtray, knowing full well its smoke was wafting toward Delgado.

A punctuated move.

"Despite our conversation a few months ago, I trust it wasn't you who did the deed . . ."

"As much as I would've like to . . ." The mere mention of Wingo's name created an angry flush, one which Braniff couldn't control or ignore. "She was nothing but a nasty bitch . . ."

"That may be—but, it's come to my attention someone is snooping in my business, and I want to know who."

"What does that have to do with McNamara?"

Delgado didn't say anything for a few moments, weighing how direct he should be with the man sitting across from him. His ultimate conclusion?

Not very.

"I don't know—maybe nothing." A pause. "But, trust me, my friend—someone's sticking his nose where it doesn't belong doesn't put us in the best position."

"Meaning?"

Delgado tried not to show his disgust at having to explain everything. "Think, Braniff—you worked for McNamara. Who do you think they're going to come after first?"

Braniff was quiet, knowing Delgado was right. It did make sense—if someone were launching a new, targeted investigation into Wingo McNamara's murder, he'd have a bullseye on his back as a person of interest. "What do you have in mind?" A pause. "And, what about Murphy? They'll come after him, too . . ."

"Probably—but, I can't do anything about him. It's you we have to protect . . ."

A lie? Of course. Protecting Murphy wasn't Delgado's job, and learning what the D.C. detective was up to had nothing to do with Rowan Murphy or anyone else.

It was about Dominic Delgado's saving his own skin.

Again, Braniff was quiet. Finally, he took a last drag on his cigarette, then ceremoniously extinguished it as if making a grand statement. "Okay—who?"

"Decklin Kilgarry."

"Do you recognize him?" Decklin glanced at Graham, then focused again on the detective's computer monitor. "I haven't been here long enough to know many . . ." He paused. "What's your gut—male?"

"Yes—but, as you can see, not a big guy. I'm not ruling out a woman, though—not yet."

Decklin nodded. "Rewind, please . . ." Again, he watched as Walsh slowed the video to frame-by-frame. "How tall is Delgado?"

"Probably about five-nine—maybe ten. Not big . . ."

"Do you think the body type in the video matches his frame?"

"Hard to tell—could be. But, both of us know the intruder could be a lot of other people, too . . ."

So, within ten and little resolved, Decklin left Walsh to other matters, both men agreeing to meet two days later in a nearby village ten miles down the road. "Shanagarry has a few out-of-sight taverns," Walsh commented as Decklin headed for the door. "With weather like this, I doubt anyone from here will be anywhere near there . . ."

"Let's hope not!"

As Decklin headed for his car, he couldn't help thinking there was something missing—such as why would anyone tail him since he was a newcomer to the village? *Because I'm a threat,* he thought as he unlocked his vehicle, reminding himself to look for something newer to buy. As much as he figured he would only be in Cobh for a short time, it was quickly becoming home, and he needed his own wheels.

Especially if he were going to give Dominic Delgado the pleasure of his company.

Contrary to what some believe, expert surveillance takes time, planning, and the ability to react in any given situation—all of which Decklin Kilgarry was a true master. Being new in town also played in his favor since few would recognize him—still, there were considerable risks.

The first thing he needed to determine was where Dominc Delgado was hanging out—and, his best guess was with the lovely Miranda. Human nature, he figured, usually didn't stray far from its roots, so spending a few evenings in the tackiest bars in town seemed the best bet. Conversation would surely reveal where Miranda usually did business, so tracking her down didn't present a problem.

Her giving up Delgado might.

Even so, he had to try, and experience told him it was best to tread lightly—spending time in one of Ireland's fine detention centers didn't exactly appeal.

As a safety precaution, Detective Walsh approved Decklin's plan, the Daft Irishman first on his list. What some may describe as a quaint drinking establishment located on a back street no one would care to stroll, the Daft offered seclusion and privacy, few caring to know anyone's name. Personal business remained as such and, if a fight or two broke out on a Saturday night?

Well, no one cared about that, either.

So, shortly after midnight, Decklin pulled on the Daft Irishman's door, the stench of stale beer greeting him as if he were an old friend. A few old salts turned to eye him as Decklin threw his coat, hat, and gloves on a table near the end of the bar, hoping to catch a private conversation without anyone's noticing. "A pint," he barked at the barkeep, making certain to keep up appearances. Moments later, he sat by himself, missing nothing as patrons went about their lives. Then?

Pay dirt.

He watched as the front door opened, a young woman making a targeted dramatic entrance. Alone, she smiled as she made her way to the bar, well aware all eyes were on her. *Probably a welcome sight*, Decklin thought as he made mental note of who paid particular interest.

But, as alluring as she undoubtedly was, most patrons only wanted to look—until Decklin took a seat next to her. "You're a sight for sore eyes," he commented, admiring her obvious assets.

"You ain't so bad yourself!"

"Drink?"

"Of course . . . "

Off and running.

Within the hour, he had her name, where he could get in touch with her other than the Daft, and a potential get-together on the table—depending, of course, on how things moved forward. That evening, Decklin opted to keep conversation casual, leaving no inkling of his interest in Dominc Delgado. From the little time he spent with her, it was clear she'd sell her own mother if it benefited her overall plan—so, Miranda's sharing an intimate, barstool conversation with Delgado would be a given.

Mentioning him was a risk Decklin wasn't willing to take. A firm believer in maneuvering situations to his benefit in an investigation, he was okay with letting his plan play out.

It was simply a matter of time.

Chapter 17

Carmine Ignatius Borja wasn't known for his patience—so, when a month passed with little to show for Dominic Delgado's efforts to learn who offed Wingo McNamara and Keegan Sullivan, alternative tactics were in order. Clearly, Delgado wasn't the man Borja thought he was and, in addition to poor performance, lack of personal grit was becoming particularly abhorrent.

Then, there was the issue of flapping jaws—more than once, it came to his attention Delgado wasn't exactly shy about strutting his masculinity whenever he could, and it was only a matter of time until satisfying his psychological and physical needs became an issue. At that moment?

They were an issue.

There was a time, of course, Carmine Borja would've taken care of such a pesky task personally—but, since his meteoric ascent up the organization's ladder, it was a pleasant change of pace to call in those who could act at his behest. "You'll be in and out," he advised, slipping his man a piece of paper. "Memorize it—then, burn it."

With only a nod, the man barely glanced at the writing, then ceremoniously placed it in the ashtray on Borja's desk. "How about if you do the honors?"

Smiling, Carmine Borja leaned forward, flicking his cigarette lighter twice before ignition. "Yes. It will be my pleasure . . ."

Miranda smiled, then sat on the bed, patting the spot beside her. "There's plenty of room . . ."

"I see that—but, honestly, I'm not feeling too well today, so I was thinking maybe we could just talk." Decklin returned the smile, albeit a wan one, to accompany his sickly performance. "Money isn't a problem . . ." Quickly, he reached into his jacket pocket, then extracted enough cash and then some to adequately cover her precious time.

"Talk?" She eyed the bills as he tossed them on the bed.

"If you don't mind—the first time I met you I knew you were a woman who could carry on an intelligent conversation. And, being on the road all the time, I miss that . . ."

"You don't seem the type to be in the Daft . . ."

"What type is that?"

"You know—and, if I didn't know better, I'd say you're not who you say you are."

"A cop?"

Miranda reached for the bills, then tucked them away just in case. "It wouldn't be the first time."

"Well, I assure you I'm not . . ." A pause. "Fishing."

"You're a fisherman?"

A nod. "I'm thinking of setting up a trawler in Cobh for the next salmon season." Another pause. "Plus, charter . . ." In that moment, he silently thanked Conner for the numerous evenings they drank Irish coffees, discussing his livelihood.

"Fishing hasn't been too good here . . ."

"You mean this last season?" Decklin sat back in his chair by the desk in her small room. "That's not what I hear."

"Well, for some, I suppose—but, there aren't nearly as many as there used to be."

"Meaning?"

A shrug. "I don't know—all I know is people are leaving."

"You mean fishermen in particular?" Decklin was quiet for a moment before asking his next question. "And, I suppose, it's affected your business, as well . . ."

"Yes."

A brief silence. "I can tell you're exactly as I thought—smart and beautiful." Decklin smiled, hoping she would be a bit more chatty. "So, Miranda—who would you go to if you were looking to start a trawler business in Cobh?"

"Well, most of the men I know aren't exactly the types to be starting their own business . . ." She paused, shifting her weight on the bed. "But, there is one . . ."

"Is he from here?"

"Not originally . . ."

"Really?" A pause. "Although, I guess that's not unusual since I'm doing the same thing!"

"Where are you from—America, I'm guessing."

"Yep—Idaho. We're known for our salmon fishing!"

Suddenly, Miranda's eyes filled with tears. "I've never been anywhere . . ."

Decklin didn't say anything for a minute, allowing her time to compose herself. Finally, he tackled the information he needed. "Do you think . . ." He hesitated, playing his part perfectly.

"Do I think what?"

"Well, I know it's a lot to ask—but, do you think I could speak with your friend about the fishing here?"

Miranda cocked her head, carefully scrutinizing everything about him. "Well, I don't see what harm it can do."

"Much appreciated. What's his name?"

"Delgado. Dominic Delgado . . ."

As Graham Walsh stared at the stubby, opaque, frozen torso sticking out of an icy snowbank, he couldn't help thinking of Ichabod Crane. *Holy shit*, he thought, as it became clear the body was meant to be nothing more than a prop for shock value. Sans its head, it was his best guess as to what lay concealed beneath the snow—and, as much as he wanted Decklin Kilgarry to see for himself, he didn't dare.

He did keep him apprised, however.

"I know it's late," he began before needing to blow his nose after spending the day in the frigid cold. "But—we have a body."

Decklin sat up in bed, instantly awake. "What?" A pause. "Who?"

"We don't know—head was lopped off, obviously before it was placed."

"Prints?"

"We haven't gotten that far. It hasn't been long . . ."

Decklin checked the clock on his cell. "It's a little after three . . . how long do you think the body's been there?"

"In this weather, who knows? Blood dripping from the neck is frozen, but the corpse isn't stiff. So, based on those two things? Not long . . ."

"What can I do to help?"

Walsh thought for a moment, instinctively knowing Decklin Kilgarry needed to stay as far away from the crime scene as possible. "Nothing. Stay clear—word will get around quickly enough. Keep your ear to the ground, and advise Connor and Alannah to do the same."

With that, Detective Walsh rang off, turning his attention to the matter at hand and, by dawn, the body was ready to be moved to the Cobh morgue. Carefully, the coroner and his team removed snow concealing the remainder of the body, everyone on the scene silent as they slowly revealed another atrocity. "Sir?" The coroner glanced at Walsh, then back at the body.

"I see, Thomas . . ."

"Both hands—they're gone. And, the legs . . ."

As two medics lifted the torso onto a waiting gurney for transport, there was no mistaking the message . . .

A 'catch me if you can' kind of thing.

"That's three within the last six months," Connor noted when Decklin delivered the news early the following morning. "What do you think?"

"Nothing, yet—it's too early." He paused. "Besides, Walsh was absolutely right when he said I couldn't be anywhere near the crime scene. If anyone happens to see me there . . ."

"I can't bear the thought of anything happening to you," Alannah blurted out as she poured three cups of coffee.

Decklin smiled, touched by her spontaneous comment. "Nothing's going to happen to me—everything I learn will need to be from Connor and you. And, Walsh . . ."

"Did Graham tell you when he'd get in touch," Connor asked, uncomfortable with the thought there was, indeed, a killer among them. "And, what about Sullivan and Wingo? Do you think it's the same killer?"

"As much as I wish I could answer your questions, I can't—we'll have to wait for the coroner's report, as well as hearing what Graham has to say."

Easier said than done.

By the end of the following week, Graham Walsh arranged a morning meeting with Decklin in Shanagarry, his reasons for a face-to-face obvious. "From what we know about Sullivan and Wingo," he advised, "it's pretty clear this isn't the same killer."

"What makes you so sure?"

"Well, for one thing, Sullivan and Wingo weren't mutilated to prevent recognition—both of us know that sort of thing brings something completely different to the table."

"True—unless we're dealing with a particularly intelligent and diabolical killer."

Walsh wasn't convinced. "Maybe—but, my gut tells me we're dealing with two killers."

"You might be right—but, doesn't it strike you odd all of a sudden there's a spate of murders in your village? There has to be a reason for it, and I submit they're connected . . ."

"Well, until there's something concrete . . ." Walsh paused, then changed the topic. "There's one other thing . . ." Hesitating, he took a sip of coffee. "When we uncovered the torso, that's exactly what it was. A torso . . ."

Decklin was silent for a moment, allowing the detective's words to sink in. "No arms?"

"Well, hands. Or, legs—sawed off with what we suspect was a chainsaw."

"Jesus!"

"Yeah—pretty gruesome."

Again, Decklin was quiet, knowing Walsh's information put them again at square one when it came to connecting the murders. "Nothing?"

Graham shook his head. "No . . ."

Just then, Walsh's cell buzzed, Decklin recognizing the familiar expression on Graham's face when reading the text. "News?"

Smiling, Graham handed his cell to Decklin so he could read it for himself. "You might say that . . . someone just discovered a hand."

Quickly, Decklin scanned the message. "You're a lucky man!" Another quick sip, then Decklin stood. "I'd say our meeting is over . . ."

Chapter 18

It was then things began to move—three murders in one town were enough to raise anyone's antennae, and villagers were getting a little antsy, demanding answers. Some wanted to call a town meeting—an idea quickly becoming much too popular—while others chose to clam up, keeping thoughts to themselves just in case they happened to be next. To say discontent was escalating to something ugly may be a little excessive—but, not by much.

While waiting for test results of the newly discovered frozen right hand, Decklin made it a point to spend a little quality time with Miranda to make certain he had the right information. "I won't take up much of your time," he commented as he offered customary payment. "But, it seems Dominic Delgado is nowhere to be found . . ."

"I know. I heard—but, that isn't unusual. Anyone who knows him isn't surprised when he takes off until the next fishing season." A pause. "It's what we do in Cobh . . ."

"So, you're not concerned?"

Suddenly, Miranda belted out a gut laugh. "Concerned? Hardly—whatever Dominic wants to do, he'll do. He's not the sort of man to be held down or beholden to anyone . . ."

Struggling to not sound like a cop, he smiled. "Well, it sure would've been nice to talk to him—I have to start making plans." A pause. "Where does he hang out when he's not in Cobh?"

"You mean where does he live?"

"Well, yes—I guess that's exactly what I mean!" Another smile.

"Spain—I don't know where."

As much as Decklin would've liked to extract more information, doing so presented unacceptable risk. "Spain?" He chuckled, pouring on the boyish charm. "Unfortunately, that's out!" Then, he stood, offering a handshake to the unwitting young woman who was trying to make a living the best way she knew how. "Perhaps, our paths will cross again . . ."

With that he was gone, certain he snagged the first clue to solving the Cobh murders, but, as he stepped onto the lamp-lit street, hair on the back of his neck began to rise as it had several weeks prior. Quickly, he scanned the dank, lonely street, then turned again to the door he just exited.

Nothing.

"I trust you have something to tell me . . ." Carmine Borja leveled a customary glare, intimidating to anyone unlucky enough to stand before him.

"Yes—but, not, perhaps, what you hoped. At least in one regard . . ."

"You have three minutes."

A quick drag. "They found a body."

"Delgado?"

"Perhaps."

"What the hell does that mean?" Borja was running low on patience, and the whole thing was beginning to get on his nerves. "I trust you carried out your mission . . ."

"I told you I'd take care of things. There was little to find—just a torso. No arms or legs—dumped in a snow bank, buried up to the neck."

Borja was quiet for a few moments, considering the situation. "Then, our hands are clean . . ." Of course, that was exactly what his man intimated moments prior, but Carmine wasn't one to laud anyone's thinking—if there were plaudits to dish out, he needed to be the recipient.

Then, he leveled a stony glare at the man who'd take a bullet for him. "Dismissed . . ."

Connections? Always a good thing, and it wasn't long before Decklin was learning all there was to know about Dominic Delgado. Hailing from Spain as Miranda indicated, his education was spotty, and it wasn't until he approached middle age did he seem to get his act together. Up until then? Petty stuff of little consequence. But, most interesting? After Delgado turned thirty-five, he disappeared from public life, happy to live his on the straight—at least, that's what it seemed.

In his gut, however, Decklin knew there was more.

After a quick call to his former partner in D.C., within hours he held a full dossier in his hands thanks to technology. "I have it," he informed Detective Walsh, the second it arrived. "My place or yours?"

Walsh chuckled as he checked his calendar. "Yours—fewer people to see me come and go." As would anyone, he, too, held a mounting concern regarding his movements. "After dark..."

"I'll be here."

Shortly before dawn, Detective Graham Walsh bid goodbye to his U.S. counterpart, both men agreeing Delgado had much to tell as well as much to hide. But, until Decklin could locate him, all the information in the world wouldn't open the book on what was really up to in Cobh. Gut feelings of both men?

Dominic Delgado was involved in the salmon poaching up to his eyeballs.

Finn Kildare stood at the end of the deserted dock, the morning sun's icy rays filling his soul. *This is where I belong*, he thought, warming his hands on his coffee mug. His next thought, however, was one of curiosity—just how many fishermen hung up their waders for the last time, many leaving the village for something a little more lucrative. No mass exodus. No goodbyes. Just picking up lives and tradition because those without scruples chose to upend everything. *Surely, there must be something we can do . . .*

It was then a seed of dark resolution began pushing its way to the top of conscious thought. Akin to Decklin's and Graham's investigation, he, too, began considering who with unknown intent entered their small village over the past few years. It was no secret fishermen from away were always regarded with a jaded eye, but, in his gut, he knew there was no one within their midst capable of betraying their own kind. Their culture.

Their livelihood.

So, as he stood thinking about what went wrong and who was to blame, there was only one person he could think of who gave him a feeling of being an outsider.

Decklin Kilgarry.

When he thought about it, there was little question it was odd someone from the Kilgarry clan showed up during such a tumultuous time in Cobh. Not only that, when he first met Kilgarry at the O'Quinn's, there was a sense of arrogance Kildare didn't particularly enjoy—although, he was aware of Decklin's effort to fit in. *Who's he to think he can solve our problems simply because he believes he can?*

It was a fair question, too. If there were one thing Finn Kildare hated more than anything, it was arrogance—and, in his mind, it dripped from Decklin Kilgarry's pores. Of course, standing on the dock in the frigid cold, he couldn't think of a reason to link Kilgarry to the murders of his mates and the unfortunate torso. Not much was being said, and there was no reason to believe that would change. It was no secret Detective Walsh was being tight-lipped about the torso's identity, and it seemed that was just fine with the villagers. As soon as astonishment—feigned, or otherwise—died down, they quickly returned to their own lives as they always did—the typical out of sight, out of mind.

Finn, however, knew differently.

Perhaps, he considered, *it's time I ramp up my own investigation. Surely, I can do better . . .*

It was, after all, the least he could do.

Grief.

When left unchecked, it destroys lives, shattered souls left to wonder when things will return to normal. It's a time when answers offer little in the way of consolation, further convincing those who are within grief's grip that their lives are changed forever.

They are.

A fact Aidan McNamara didn't want to admit.

The truth was blatant animosity between his daughter and him was water under the piers, making no difference as he and his wife tried to glue together fractured pieces of their lives. A lofty goal—and, unfortunately, nothing they tried was working. As far as they knew, no one was doing a damned thing about their daughter's murder, leaving both to think no one cared—a definite possibility.

Another thing Wingo's father didn't want to consider.

With renewed vigor, he pulled on his boots, grabbed his jacket from the hook by the door, then called to his wife. "I'll be back soon, luv . . ."

Quickly, he pulled the cottage door closed, stepping into Cobh's mercurial weather before she could ask where he was going. *It's better this way . . .*

Head tucked against offshore wind as he walked to his truck, within twenty he stood at Graham Walsh's office door. Briefly, as he watched Walsh scribble something on a legal pad through his office window, he considered leaving—yet, he knew it was time.

He rapped on the window, offering only a broken smile of a man who lost one of his own.

"Aidan!" Walsh grinned and stood, gesturing for the aging fisherman to make himself comfortable as he opened the door. "I didn't expect to see you!"

"Aye! I didn't expect to see you until I knew I had to . . ."

A comment Walsh chose to ignore. "Have a seat!" He waited as Aidan shrugged off his coat, then sat in a worn chair in front of the detective's desk. "Now, what brings you to my side of the village?"

Aidan fiddled with the bottom edge of his sweater, eyes cast to the floor, not knowing quite what to say. "I'm here about Erin . . ."

"Wingo."

A nod. "The missus and I need to know . . ."

"I wish . . ."

Aidan sighed, one deep enough to embrace his troubled soul. "We seldom got along, you know . . ."

Walsh said nothing, waiting for him to continue, knowing anything he said would ring empty.

"When she was a wee one, she pestered me to take her fishing until I couldn't say no—more out of self-preservation, I'd say, than my wanting her on the boat." Aidan paused, recalling the hurt he must have heaped on his daughter. "She knew, too . . ."

"Knew what?"

"She knew I couldn't love her like I could my own son."

"But, you don't have . . ."

Aidan looked up. "That's my point."

Silence.

Finally, Graham took advantage of the situation. "Is there anything you can tell me about Wingo's—Erin's—friends? You know, who she hung out with when she wasn't fishing . . ." Of course, within hours of finding Wingo's body, Graham spoke with both of her parents, neither having any idea of who could do such a thing.

"That's just it—you know my daughter was a loudmouth who said anything she wanted to anyone, at any time. I don't think it's a stretch to say she had enemies . . ."

"Any idea of who they might be?"

Aidan shook his head. "No—from away, no doubt."

"You mean fisherman who were only in Cobh for the season?"

A nod. "Everyone around here knows what Erin was like—and, I can't bring myself to believe one of us would have anything to do with it!"

Walsh sat back in his chair, not taking his eyes from the old man sitting across from him. When he thought about it, Aidan McNamara had a point—if there were one thing Graham knew about his village, it was locals supported locals. "Anyone in particular?"

"No—but, I have my suspicions."

If it were anyone else, Detective Graham Walsh would've advised spitting it out and getting on with it. "If there's anything I need to know, Aidan, now's the time . . ."

Another nod coupled with momentary silence. "I didn't meet him . . ."

"Who?"

"I never knew his name—but, he's the reason my daughter was having such a good season."

"I heard—she was talking about buying another trawler."

"Not with my blessing!" Aidan reached in his pocket for a worn handkerchief, swiped at his nose, then tucked it back in his pocket. "Foolishness! Absolute foolishness!"

"Why? If she had the money, why shouldn't she invest it in our community?"

Again, silence.

Graham leaned forward. "What do you need to tell me, Aidan?"

Suddenly, Aidan McNamara stood, grabbed his coat, then headed for Walsh's office door. "I shouldn't have come!"

Now, had that been any other day, Graham Walsh would've let him go, knowing the stress Aidan was enduring. That day?

Not on his life.

"Aidan!"

The fisherman turned, eyes glistening with tears laced with painful recollection.

"Aidan, please. Let's talk . . ."

Gently, Graham guided him back to his seat, drawing up a folding chair directly across from him. "Tell me . . ."

Aidan's voice caught as he recalled the last time he spoke to his daughter. "We argued . . ."

"About?"

"The trawler."

"Wingo's existing trawler, or the new one she wanted to buy?"

"The new one—she said money was no object." Aidan paused, thinking. "How can that be, Graham? Our lives are always about money, and not having enough of it!"

"Was someone giving her extra cash?"

A nod. "Had to be." Then, Aidan McNamara focused on Cobh's long-serving detective. "She sold her soul to the devil, Walsh. I'm sure of it—the money was dirty."

"Who, Aidan?" A pause as he watched McNamara grapple with his supposed truth. "Who was the devil?"

Just then, Aidan straightened a little—as much as he could—his chin set with parental resolve. "Like I said, I don't know his name. All I know is a mole was on my daughter's boat . . ."

"A mole? Why do you think so?"

"How else would she have a connection to money?"

A valid point—the chances of Wingo McNamara's knowing whom to go to when it came to bailing her out of a disastrous season had to be someone close. Someone who knew she was on the brink of losing everything. "She had three deckhands, as I recall . . ."

A nod. "One had been with her for a couple of seasons—the other two were new."

"What do you think, Aidan—who was the mole?"

"The quiet one . . ."

"Name?"

"Smokey . . ."

Chapter 19

As much as Graham Walsh didn't like involving anyone in an investigation other than trained personnel, it was clear he had little choice. "I need your help," he told Connor O'Quinn as he pulled out a chair at the O'Quinn's kitchen table. "Is Decklin coming?"

"Aye—he should be here shortly." Connor paused, slightly unnerved by Walsh's showing up on his doorstep, unannounced. "Care to tell me what this is about?"

Graham smiled. "Sorry for sounding so secretive—but, I think I got a solid lead in Wingo's murder this afternoon."

Before Connor could speak, Decklin appeared, Alannah behind him, smiling. "Look what the cat dragged in," she laughed as she headed to the stove to put on a pot of tea.

Within minutes, they sat at the table, ready to hear what Detective Walsh had on his mind. "This afternoon," he began, "Aidan McNamara came to see me . . ."

Connor glanced at Decklin. "What about?"

"At first, I wasn't sure, but when he showed up at my office door, it was clear he was a man with something on his mind."

"He wanted to discuss his daughter's murder, I'm guessing . . ." Decklin kept his focus on Walsh, certain of Aidan's reason for visiting the detective.

"Yes—but, it wasn't what you may think." Walsh paused, recalling his conversation with Wingo's father. "He thinks Wingo sold her soul to someone from away to make as much money as she could on the trawler . . ."

Connor's eyebrows arched north. "Sold her soul? To whom?"

"Well, that's the thing—he's not sure." Again, he paused, knowing his next words were going to blow their minds. "But, he suspects there was a mole on her boat . . ."

Alannah gasped. "A mole? What does that mean?"

Decklin's turn. "It's someone who listens to everything, then reports to the person who's paying him—or, her."

"In other words," her husband offered, "selling her out."

"But, why Wingo," Alannah asked. "Why would anyone be interested in her? That doesn't make sense!"

"It does," Decklin suggested, "if she needed money."

"But, everyone here is in the same boat! All of us are suffering! So, why would someone choose her for . . ." Alannah paused, realizing she had no idea why anyone would target Wingo McNamara.

Detective Walsh took a sip of tea, then placed his cup on its saucer. "Aidan thinks one of her deckhands was keeping an eye on everything, reporting back to someone how much they were catching—which, in turn, translates into how much Wingo was making. After paying her deckhands and other operating costs, it couldn't have been much . . ."

"So," Connor interjected, "you're saying the only reason Wingo was making money toward the end of the season was because . . ."

"She was fishing illegally—and, knew it."

"Illegally? Where?"

Walsh shook his head, then took another warm sip. "I don't know—I didn't get that far with the conversation. It was difficult enough for Aidan to talk about it, let alone consider the fact his daughter was caught up in something . . .'

"Nefarious?" Decklin glanced at them, realizing they were about to take their investigation in a new direction.

"Exactly."

"Who's the mole? Did he say?"

A smile. "Indeed, he did." A pause. "A deckhand everyone calls 'Smokey.'"

"I know him," Connor advised, a look of disgust crossing his face. "Never says much—but, the one or two times I met him on Wingo's trawler, I wasn't impressed."

Walsh grinned. "I don't think Aidan is too impressed with him, either . . ."

"So," Alannah asked, "what's the next step? Haul him in for questioning?"

Walsh and Decklin chuckled, enjoying her innocence about such things. "Well, not quite," Decklin offered. Then, he turned to Detective Walsh. "What are you going to do?"

Graham was quiet for a moment, then drained his tea cup. "I'm not sure—but, there's one other thing." A momentary silence. "Aidan believes there's someone else involved . . ."

Decklin nodded. "The person a few rungs up the ladder."

"Precisely—so, who's paying for what?"

First order of business?

Ramp up the investigation despite what anyone says—on the QT, of course. So, by the end of the week, Detective Graham Walsh decided to interrogate every deckhand working the previous salmon season—without offering an opportunity to decline. First up?

Smokey.

It was only by a stroke of luck Walsh learned Wingo's deckhand was wandering about town, although no one who spotted him knew exactly why. Fishing didn't begin for another few months, and anyone who knew of him was clear on the fact Smokey thought Cobh was nothing more than a two-bit village, offering nothing except a little extra jingle in his pocket. *If that's what he thinks*, Walsh considered, *why is he wasting his time here? The money can't be that good . . .*

Thoughts, of course, leading to the realization perhaps more money was being doled out than originally figured.

And, it was immediately after that thought, Detective Walsh's cell phone buzzed, rewarding his investigative efforts with long-awaited news. "Dominic Delgado," the voice commented as soon as Walsh answered. "The right hand. It belongs to Dominic Delgado . . ."

After a quick thank you, Walsh rang Decklin. "It's him," he advised. "The hand belongs to Delgado . . ."

Finally.

If there were more than a few McNamaras left in the village, someone surely would've had a fight on their hands when it came to dealing with who murdered the seasoned trawler captain—and, Keegan Sullivan, if it happened they were connected. As it was, Aidan, his wife, and Wingo's cousin on her mother's side were the only remnants of family willing to get involved, effectively leaving it up to Wingo's father to exact appropriate revenge.

As much as Aidan hoped Detective Walsh was doing his best, there was more than one reason he wanted to discuss his daughter's murder in person. During private moments steeped in sorrow and isolation, Aidan McNamara couldn't still the thought Wingo's murder was covered up for a reason—and, if that were the case, who was calling the shots?

A disturbing question he couldn't put to rest.

Surely, Aidan thought, *Detective Walsh was as much in the dark as anyone else* . . .

But, the thought Walsh could've done more, lingered—probably because there wasn't anyone else to blame. Still, pulling the plug on two fresh murder investigations didn't seem to be Walsh's style. *That means*, Aidan figured as he stoked the last fire for the last time that evening, *someone ordered him to back off—or, paid him.*

Jabbing at fading embers with a poker, it became clear no one was really up to the job of finding out who murdered his daughter—a situation leaving him in the position of deciding something his wife would undoubtedly hate. Even so, making things right seemed the only thing to do . . .

Didn't it?

Decklin pulled on the Daft's door, not exactly sure if he wanted to show his face again—twice allowed him the luxury of being forgettable. Three times?

Old friends.

In his favor was the fact it was Saturday night, most patrons drunk on their collective asses by the time the clock struck midnight. After that?

All Decklin could hope for was someone chatty.

Easing through a group of drunken fishermen, he spied a small table tucked into the corner, perfect for keeping an eye on the Daft Irishman's comings and goings. Moving the chair so his back was to the wall, the dark corner was perfect for assessing who might rally his interest simply by looks or words. His true target, however?

Smokey Alvera.

If he were, in fact, gracing the streets of Cobh before fishing season, it wasn't exactly a stretch to think the Daft might be a tavern of choice. Unfortunately, all Decklin had to go on was a description, one not instilling a modicum of confidence—identification based on little more than gut feeling. And, of course, the possibility someone may call out Smokey's name . . .

But, Decklin wasn't holding his breath.

Chapter 20

*T*here's a certain sense of satisfaction when a plan comes together—you know, unbridled exhilaration coupled with too much self-congratulatory chest-puffing. It's a feeling most enjoy when opportunity presents itself, many wishing to languish in the rush of realizing their true worthiness for as long as possible.

And, Finn Kildare was one of them.

With fishing season underway, he pulled up a chair to his workbench, assessing what tools and fishing gear needed replacing, if any.

Since Wingo McNamara was out of the picture, her demise—as unfortunate as it was—left opportunity for those who were bold enough to take it. For those who weren't?

Well, the new season probably wouldn't be much different than the last.

Although it was nearly midnight, with loving reverence he inspected all rods and reels, noting which were needing replacement, as well as fishing line that may be good for one more season. *This year,* he thought as he felt for thinning in the line with his fingertips, *I'm heading back to ancestral waters* . . . Waters his great-grandfather and every Kildare after him fished to put food on the table with a little left over. Of course, he'd been there during prior seasons, but with little to show for his efforts, he back-burnered family fishing grounds in place of something more promising.

Then, as always, the issue of responsible deckhands cropped up, somehow managing to piss him off before he even considered who he'd hire for the season. There was something about Rowan Murphy he didn't quite trust, but with three murders looming over the village, they may be enough of a deterrent to affect the overall deckhand candidate pool. *If I have to,* he thought, changing gears as he considered possibilities, *I'll keep him* . . .

With the next thought, he recalled Wingo McNamara's deckhands were, most likely, out of a job and, having met Smokey only once, there was little to know or like. A strong set of hands and a modicum of smarts were the only prerequisites to work as a deckhand, and Finn didn't really care about them other than the fact they could sling fish guts and bait with the best of them.

Wingo's other deckhand? *Braniff,* Finn considered, *doesn't quite seem to fit in with the other hands* . . . In Finn's mind, there wasn't much to know or consider—there was also something about Braniff he didn't like or trust, and the thought of having Wingo's former deckhand on his boat was nothing less than repugnant—in fact, he was as distasteful as his former boss.

So, as he rifled through fishing gear, readying for the upcoming season, it seemed Finn Kildare had a few decisions to make regarding his livelihood. But, there was one other thing needing his attention . . .

What the hell Decklin Kilgarry was really doing in Cobh.

Decklin watched as fishermen came and went, most staying for only a pint or two, ultimately making their way back to wherever. As he suspected, the Daft wasn't exactly hopping, the hope of snagging a conversation with Smokey fading as the tavern emptied. The good news?

Miranda was working.

"Well," she commented after spying him sitting alone in the corner. "What brings you here? I didn't think I'd see you again . . ."

In Decklin's mind?

Opportunity just knocked.

"I was hoping I'd catch you," Decklin commented with a smile as he rose, then pulled out the adjacent chair. "I want to extend my condolences . . ."

Suddenly, Miranda's eyes filled with tears. "I couldn't believe it when I heard about Dominic! Who would do such a thing?"

"I have no idea—I haven't been here long enough to know very many people." A pause. "Who do you think did it, Miranda? You seemed to know Delgado pretty well—did he ever talk about anyone?"

Taking her time to think for a few moments, she finally shook her head. "No—he didn't really talk about anyone he knew other than some of the hands at the dock."

"Anyone in particular?"

"Well, he mentioned Smokey a few times—but, I don't remember what he said. That was last season . . ."

It was all Decklin could do to not pull out the tiny, spiral notepad from his jacket pocket. "Smokey—he was a deckhand?"

Miranda nodded. "I think he worked for Wingo McNamara, but I'm not sure . . ."

"Anyone else?"

Momentary silence. "No, not really—the only other name I remember is Carmine. But, honestly, I have no idea who he is . . ."

"You've never heard the name before? Around the village, I mean . . ."

"No."

"Did you ever have an opportunity to meet Smokey? He must've been in here a few times . . ."

"I saw him, but Dominic never introduced us . . ."

"Were Dominic and Smokey here together?" As if a subliminal cue, Decklin scanned the nearly empty bar to make sure no one was paying attention to their conversation.

"Sometimes—whenever Dominic was with someone, I had strict orders not to pay him any mind."

Decklin watched her carefully, noting the hurt in her eyes. "Like I said, I'm sorry—is there anyone you need to contact? You know—about Dominic?"

Miranda thought for a second, then shook her head. "Not really—the only person he ever mentioned was someone named Carmine."

"A friend?"

"I don't know—he never said."

"If Carmine is in Cobh, I imagine he knows by now . . ."

Again, Miranda shook her head. "No, I don't think so. I'm pretty sure Dominic knew him from where he lived in Spain . . ."

Jackpot.

"Well, maybe they were childhood friends—but, it does make me wonder. If that's the case, he probably doesn't know his friend was murdered . . ."

"I don't know . . ." Then, Miranda straightened, eyeing Decklin. "Are you sure you're not a cop?"

A grin. "I'm sure." Decklin stood, grabbing his coat. "Well, I have work to do in the morning, so I better get my beauty sleep . . ." As he started to go, he suddenly turned. "Do you have a piece of paper?"

Without saying a word, she handed him a paper napkin from the table. "Will this do?"

A nod. Quickly he scribbled something, then handed it to her. "If I can ever do anything for you . . ." With that, he was gone.

Miranda unfolded the napkin as she glanced at the door.

Decklin
011 353 1 482 9781

When thoughts of dirty money begin to mingle with suspicion, it's never a good sign—and, Graham Walsh knew it. "Are you sure," he asked, switching his cell to his other ear.

"Positive—it didn't happen." The voice on the other end paused. "What's going on up there, Walsh?"

"I don't know—but, I'm sure as hell going to find out." With that he clicked off, thoughts of what his colleague just told him still front and center. Silently chastising himself for not investigating as soon as the two detectives from Ireland's Special Detective Unit showed up to investigate Keegan Sullivan's murder, what he just learned derailed everything.

I met with both of them, Graham thought, recalling his conversations. *Neither gave any indication they weren't who they said they were* . . . And, the more he thought, the more pissed he became. It's never a good thing when someone pulls the wool—and, to someone within the law?

Not smart.

Quickly, he pulled his cell from his pocket, tapping the screen three times. Then, a connection. "Kilgarry?" Walsh didn't wait for confirmation. "We have a problem . . ."

Instantly, Decklin recognized the urgency in his voice. "What's up?"

For the next ten, Detective Walsh recounted his conversation with a higher-up of Ireland's Special Detective Unit, finally wrapping it up with a grunt. "I'll be damned if they'll get away with this, Kilgarry . . ."

"Had you ever seen the men prior to the time they showed up after Sullivan's murder?"

"No—and, I'd remember if I had. But, in my own defense, I know only a handful of detectives in the Unit—and, that's only because of training meetings. You know . . ."

"Did they show you their credentials?"

Silent for a moment, Detective Walsh recalled when he first learned the men were in town. "Of course—everything looked good."

Decklin, too, was quiet as he considered what Walsh just told him. There was something in his voice that didn't ring true, even though Decklin hadn't known him long. "You're sure?"

Another silence. "Well, yes—although, I admit I wasn't as diligent as I should've been." It was then Detective Walsh felt an embarrassing flush creep into his cheeks, grateful Decklin couldn't see. "I made a mistake."

"Do you recall their names?"

"I wish I did . . ." From Walsh's tone, there was no doubt he was beating himself up for not doing his best work. "Spilled milk," he commented, knowing he couldn't take time to feel sorry for himself. "But, this information offers another direction . . ."

"Agreed—the question is who wanted to meddle in your investigation?"

"And, why . . ."

"Exactly—if I recall correctly, it didn't take too long for them to show up after finding Sullivan's body—so, word must've traveled fast."

Graham was quiet, thinking. "There had to be someone here, in Cobh, who was keeping an eye on everything that was happening . . ."

"And, reporting back to someone." Decklin grabbed his notebook from his jacket pocket as Walsh agreed. "The only name I haven't investigated yet is someone named 'Carmine.' Ring a bell?"

"No—then again, there are mostly locals in this village of Irish descent. 'Carmine' sounds Italian . . ."

"Or, Spanish."

As the words came out of Decklin's mouth, instinctively he knew the next step of their investigation. "Is it in your budget to take a little trip," he asked, certain he was on the right track.

"To where?"

"Spain . . ."

By noon the following day, both men dutifully presented their passports after stepping onto Spanish soil. Minutes later, they exited the airport, both certain they were on the trail of who could provide answers regarding the murders of Keegan Sullivan and Wingo McNamara. "Delgado had to be working for Carmine . . ." Detective Walsh paused, wishing they had a first name. "There's nothing else right now that makes sense."

"Yes—but, both of us know Barcelona isn't small. The chance of our finding this guy is next to nil . . ."

Unfortunately, Walsh agreed. "We have to try—with Barcelona on the coast, at least we have docks. Someone may know something—but, I'm not holding my breath." He scanned the area for a taxi as they stepped into a warm, Spanish sun. Then, he turned to Decklin. "I could kick myself for being so stupid."

"I know—I've been there. But, now we're on the right track, so let's make the best of our time here."

Grateful for his American colleague's understanding, Graham nodded. "Agreed . . ."

"At least we're here during salmon season," Decklin commented as they approached the Barcelona docks. "A lot busier than Cobh . . ."

Walsh grinned. "Aye—we're small potatoes compared to this!" Both men scanned what seemed never-ending trawlers and ships in the Barcelona Harbor. "At least," Walsh continued, "we're not too far from the working man's port."

"Meaning?"

"Well, it seems we'll probably get more information from someone who might know of our elusive Carmine." A pause. "Although, it wouldn't hurt to cruise by where the rich folks dock their yachts—my gut tells me Carmine isn't hurting for cash."

"Not to mention it's only conjecture he and Delgado were working together—what if there's more than one?"

"You mean more than one Delgado?"

"In a figurative sense—what if Carmine has more than one person working in Cobh to disrupt our fishing business." Decklin stopped, scanning the docks. "And, we can't forget about Smokey—as much as Aidan McNamara thinks he's a mole, we have no evidence."

Both men aware of the near impossibility of their task, again they set out, walking docks at the port, speaking with whomever they could, asking about Dominic Delgado.

Bupkis.

Until Decklin spied a small trawler reminding him of Wingo's rig. "Let's try this one . . ."

Without waiting for an answer, he strode toward the trawler, Walsh scanning the area behind him, keeping a wary eye. A few minutes later, they stood beside the Sea Nymph, a spotless, well-respected Spanish trawler. "Come aboard," Walsh yelled to a young deckhand swabbing the deck.

The deckhand stopped, glancing to see if anyone else were around to grant the request. Seeing no one, he gestured to them to board. "What can I do for ya," he asked in broken English, leaning on the mop handle.

"Well," Walsh began, "I'm hoping you can give us some information . . ."

The deckhand eyed both men. "About?"

"Fishing in Ireland." Walsh and Decklin agreed before they hit the docks to not mention their true intent—too risky.

"Ireland? What do I know about Ireland?" The deckhand grinned, a smile complete with two missing teeth.

"It's not too far away," Walsh laughed. "We're here looking for able-bodied deckhands for our season."

"Salmon?"

A nod—then, he gestured to Decklin. "My partner and I are short a hand or two . . ."

The deckhand eyed them. "For the whole season?"

Another nod. "Aye—do you know anybody?"

A momentary silence. "Well, now, I just might . . ."

Graham and Walsh let him think for a moment, then offered a little nudge. "We heard of a hand named 'Smokey' who may be interested—is he around? Do you know him?"

"Smokey?" The deckhand chuckled, then dipped the mop in a bucket, swiping the deck with disinterest. "Everybody knows him . . ."

Decklin's turn. "Really? Do you know where we can find him—it's getting late to bring on new hands, and we need at least two."

"From what I hear, he's already there . . ."

"In Ireland?" Walsh glanced at Decklin. "You're sure?"

"Sí—he goes there every year." The deckhand stopped mopping, focusing on both men. "I don't know where . . ."

After a few more inconsequential questions, Walsh and Decklin bade the deckhand goodbye, wishing him luck in the coming season. "Well, at least it was something," Decklin commented. "We know Smokey spends a good bit of time in our neck of the woods . . ."

"It seems so—but, we knew that," Graham commented as he watched a black sedan pull up to the same dock they just left. "Check this out . . ."

Instinctively backing as far out of sight as they could, both watched as a short, stubby, well-dressed man stepped from the car, then headed for the same trawler Walsh and Decklin just departed. "Doesn't quite seem like the type to be hanging around the docks," Decklin commented.

"Exactly what I was thinking . . ." Knowing something was off, they watched as the man boarded the trawler, said something to the deckhand, then vanished. Minutes later, he emerged, his gait one of a man on a mission. "He's pissed . . ."

"Who is this guy," Decklin muttered, knowing he was watching something unfold directly related to their case. "Eyes on the license plate . . ."

Graham nodded as both men watched the sedan speed away moments later. "See what you can find out on your end, if you don't mind. Your sources are greater than mine . . ."

Chapter 21

Carmine Borja sat at his desk, puffing on a cigar. If there were one thing he despised, it was loose ends—and, Dominic Delgado's unfortunate demise was definitely a loose end. Of course, never one to accept responsibility for anything south of the law, in his mind, it was time to take matters into his own hands. There's no one I can trust," he commented to his number one man.

"What about Smokey? He's always been loyal . . ."

"Maybe—but, he's also been stupid." A pause as Borja recalled his conversation with the young deckhand on the Spanish trawler earlier in the day. "Someone's getting too close . . ."

"Who?"

"If I knew that, I could take care of this whole situation myself!" Shooting a glare at his man sitting in his customary seat, it was clear Carmine Borja wasn't in the mood for ideas. "But, I assure you—whoever it is won't be around for long."

Although knowing his next question could possibly get him dismissed, Borja's man took what could've been an unnecessary risk. "How do you know?"

"How I know is none of your business!" An irritated puff. "Don't ever question what I know . . ." Finally, Borja focused his full attention on his man. "Get your ass to Ireland, and find out who's sticking their nose in my business . . ."

Without a word, Borja's first in command stood, pivoted like a soldier, then headed for the door.

"And, don't come back until you have something!"

"At least it's something," Decklin reported to Connor and Alannah after returning from his brief trip. "Have you seen Smokey around the docks?"

Connor shook his head. "No—but, we're just beginning the season, and it's possible all deckhands aren't in Cobh yet."

"Are you sure he's here," Alannah asked, intrigued by the topic of conversation.

"One hundred percent? No. But, my gut tells me Smokey and Carmine whoever-he-is have something in common—not only that, a Spanish deckhand said Smokey is already in Ireland."

"And, you don't have any idea of Carmine's last name?"

"No—however, I should be hearing from my guy in the States. Before we left Spain, I contacted him to see if he could send me all the information he can dig up . . ."

"Without a last name?"

Decklin smiled, enjoying his cousin's innocence when life dished up something unpleasant. "He'll know the last name because of the license plate . . ."

Alannah blushed slightly. "Oh. Yeah . . ."

Just as Decklin was about to explain more, his cell buzzed, its screen revealing the caller. "Mason! What do you have for me?" Plucking his pen and notebook from his shirt pocket, he scribbled a few lines, thanked the caller, then severed the connection. "Got it! Our mystery man is none other than Carmine Borja . . ."

Connor grinned, knowing Decklin would be hot on Borja's trail. "Things are looking up!"

"How long ago?"

"Only a few weeks . . ." Miranda eyed the man standing in front of her, unease beginning to show. "Why?"

"Why?" Suddenly the man clocked her with a powerful blow to her face. "Don't ever ask why!"

Instinctively, Miranda stepped back, her left palm cradling her cheek. "I'm sorry . . ."

Silence.

"Now, let's try this again . . ." A pause. "Who was asking questions?"

"I don't remember his name . . ." A lie? Of course.

As she answered, the man stepped closer. "Perhaps, I didn't make myself clear . . ." Again, he struck her, drawing blood from her nose.

"Wait! I have something . . ." Miranda reached for a rag on the small bureau, then dabbed her nose. Quickly, she rifled through a drawer, extracted a folded napkin, then handed it to the man. "Here . . ."

Unfolding it impatiently, he glanced at the writing, memorizing it instantly—then, he smacked her again.

You know—one more for the road.

Aidan McNamara stood on the deck of his trawler, wondering if fishing were still worth it. Age staking its claim, bones were creaking, and he no longer felt the joy of being on the water. *Maybe it's time*, he thought as he inspected his nets, thoughts of his daughter ever-present.

"Aidan! Aidan McNamara!"

The vintage fisherman turned, recognizing the voice. "What can I do for ya, Finn?"

"Permission to come aboard?"

Aidan nodded, curious as to why Finn Kildare needed to speak to him. "I ask again—what can I do for ya?"

"Well . . ." Finn Kildare stepped on board, then shifted his weight slightly to get his sea legs due to a chop on the water. "I just wanted to see if there's anything you need. I didn't pay my proper respects when . . ."

"Since when, Finn?" As if a spigot turned on, anger began to surge. "You weren't so concerned when my daughter was found dead in the water, were ya?"

"I . . ."

Aidan glared at him. "You know what I need, Finn? I need to know who did it! I need to know who murdered my Erin!" He paused, swiping his mouth with his sleeve to clear a renegade bit of spit. "But, I bet you don't have that information, do ya?"

Of course, Aidan's grief was understandable—no man should have to lose his child. "It just so happens, I may . . ."

Wingo's father sniffled, again making the best use of his sleeve. "Well? What is it?"

"Not now. I'll come to your place this evening . . ."

"You'll do no such thing," Aidan warned, his voice a raspy whisper. "I'll not have my wife upset any more than she already is . . ."

"I understand. Where, then?"

"Right here! Right now! If you've got somethin' to say, Finn Kildare, then damned well say it!"

As Finn stood before what he considered a broken man, he realized he could no longer stay silent. "I believe Wingo died at the hands of one of her deckhands."

From his tone, Aidan knew Kildare was serious. "Who?"

"Smokey—I don't know his last name."

Instantly, McNamara recalled his conversation with Graham Walsh. "Yes—he worked for Erin."

"How about we step into the wheelhouse, Aidan—it's cold."

With a nod, Aidan opened the wheelhouse door, standing aside as Finn stepped across the threshold. "Tell me what you know . . ."

A man who usually followed his intuition, Decklin Kilgarry watched as Aidan McNamara greeted his early morning guest. Why Decklin decided to conduct such an early surveillance, he wasn't sure—but, something awakened him just before sunrise, Aidan McNamara on his mind. A nudge?

Decklin thought so.

From what Detective Walsh told him about Aidan McNamara's impromptu visit days prior, the conversation needed more attention. And, when mentally dissecting the situation as he watched Finn Kildare board Aidan's trawler, one thing became clear . . .

Anyone possibly associated with Carmine Borja—or involved with Keegan Sullivan and Wingo McNamara—were in his crosshairs.

During Decklin's quick trip to Spain, Connor and Alannah did their parts by listening to village gossip, as well as paying attention to those who didn't seem to fit in.

And, it paid off.

"I was standing in line at the chemist's," Alannah began when Decklin visited the O'Quinns after his return, "and, all of a sudden, I heard someone coughing behind me." She paused, recalling the scene. "I only needed to pick up my package and he sounded like he needed help, so I let him go in front of me."

"When? What time was it," Decklin asked, scribbling a few lines on his notepad.

"It was Tuesday, right after lunch . . ."

More scribbling. "Okay—then what?"

"Well, I listened to his conversation with the chemist and, when the chemist asked his name, he said, "Alvera."

Connor glanced at Decklin, then focused again on his wife. "That's it?"

"Of course, that's not it!" Alannah shot him a look most husbands prefer to avoid. "Then, he said, 'Everyone calls me 'Smokey.'" With a triumphant look, she sat back in her chair, waiting. "Well? Did you hear what I just said?"

Decklin laughed. "We did, and excellent work, Alannah!"

Connor, too, praised his wife, then turned his attention to Decklin. "So, now we have a last name . . ."

"Indeed, we do!"

So, for the next hour, the O'Quinns and a Kilgarry from away sat at the kitchen table, discussing what was next, Alanna providing a full-blown description from height and weight to approximate age.

"Well, first," Decklin finally commented, "I need to talk to Graham, and he'll probably want to talk to you, Alannah. After that, he and I will figure out a plan . . ."

Twenty-four hours later?

Detective Decklin Kilgarry was back in the saddle, taking matters into his own hands by keeping eyes on the dock. First up?

Finn Kildare.

Twenty minutes into Decklin's first official surveillance regarding the untimely murders of Keegan Sullivan, Wingo McNamara, and Dominic Delgado, Kildare disembarked the trawler, a scowl on his face. *Judging from his expression,* the D.C. detective thought, *it looks as if things didn't go so well.*

Not well, at all . . .

The call rang in on his secondary cell precisely at midnight, rousing him from a deep sleep—after keeping Kildare within his sights during the past few days, he finally needed to catch up on rest. "Decklin."

"It's Miranda."

"Miranda—is everything alright?" Instantly awake, he flicked on the light on his nightstand, listening intently to every word.

"I . . ." A pause. "Yes, I'm fine."

"You don't sound fine—tell me. Did something happen?"

It was then she broke, heaving sobs wracking her body. "I have to warn you . . ."

"Warn me? About what?"

"I don't know his name . . ."

Decklin was quiet as he listened—though wrested from a deep sleep, he was awake enough to recognize a plea for help. "Where are you?"

"My place."

"I'm on my way . . ."

Another sob. "No! No! You can't! He may be watching!"

Grabbing his notepad and pen, Decklin sat up, then turned to a blank page. "Who? Who's watching?"

"Like I said, I don't know his name—but, I had to give him your number. The one you wrote on the napkin . . ."

Then, the question he didn't want to ask. "Did he hurt you?"

Nothing, but a softened sob.

Asked, and answered.

Chapter 22

After Miranda's surprise call, Decklin lost no time getting in touch with Graham Walsh to set up an early morning meeting. "Things are starting to break," he confided as he handed the detective a cup of coffee. "Our players are beginning to surface . . ."

"Aye—players we barely or didn't consider."

"Well, I have to be honest—it never occurred to me Miranda may be involved other than irregular dalliances with Dominic Delgado." He paused, briefly wondering if he were losing his touch. "I should've picked up on it . . ."

"Like you told me, my friend, don't beat yourself up about it—move on." Graham smiled, then took a sip. "So, what do we know?"

Both men reached for their notepads. "Okay," Decklin began, "we know Miranda most likely had the shit beaten out of her."

"The question is why . . ."

"Probably the same old, same old—somebody thought she had information about something."

"Or, somebody—but, why now?"

Decklin took a few notes, then continued. "Good question." A pause. "Did Miranda also have a working relationship with Smokey Alvera?" A pause. "Of course, we don't know, but it's something to consider . . ."

"You mean Miranda may be a plant?"

"Well, it makes sense, don't you think? Who would know to contact her to obtain needed information?"

"Someone who's keeping an eye on things . . ."

"Exactly—someone who's higher up the organizational ladder than Smokey Alvera."

"Borja."

"Bingo."

"So, Smokey Alvera works for Carmine Borja . . ."

"And, I think Delgado did, too. It makes sense—what we don't know, however, is the middleman. Who did Borja send to beat the crap out of a saloon girl trying to make a living?"

Graham took another sip of coffee, then placed the mug on the table. "The great question in my mind?"

Decklin said nothing, arching his eyebrows.

"Obviously, Borja ordered his guy to shake her down for information—but, why?" Walsh continued, not waiting for an answer. "Because someone is getting a little too close. That's what I think . . ."

"And, the only people snooping around is us . . ."

"Aye—and, now, whoever slapped Miranda around, has your phone number."

With that knowledge hanging in the air, both men felt a heaviness not previously a part of their investigation. "Then, it's a good thing it's a throwaway," Decklin finally commented. "I'll put a trace on the call if it comes in—if it originates from a burner phone, it'll be more difficult, but it can be done. If it's a personal cell, all the better for us . . ."

Graham grinned, shaking his head. "You think they'll be that stupid?"

"Who knows? We can only hope—but, whoever has the number will need to call to find out who answers.

"I suppose it does work out better for us in the long run, but I still don't like the idea of Carmine Borja's having access to you—it's a dangerous situation."

Decklin was quiet, thinking about the Pandora's Box that was about open. "I'm ready."

"I hope so . . ."

With more than four weeks of the new fishing season under their belts, again there was little success for most who were on the water. Weather precluded the promise of a good catch and, already, spirits were tanking.

Same with the investigation—until Aidan McNamara decided to divulge the content of his trawler conversation with Finn Kildare to Detective Walsh. "Somethin' don't smell right," he commented. "Why would Finn Kildare—especially now—warn me about Smokey? Why wouldn't he tell me sooner he thinks Alvera's responsible for Erin's murder?"

"Maybe he was just being kind—you know, watching out for you."

"Finn Kildare?" A brief pause. "You haven't been here as long as I have and, I can tell you, without doubt, Finn Kildare is anything but a damned choir boy . . ."

"Someone else mentioned the same thing—said Kildare was quite a handful during school years." There was no way in hell Graham was going to divulge Decklin's conversation with Alannah months prior—with three dead, he didn't want to make it four.

"Whoever told you that is right—and, after what I've witnessed over the years, it doesn't take much to set him off."

"What sets him off?"

"Poaching—in fact, I always suspected he had Keegan Sullivan workin' fer him. Under the table, of course . . ."

"For what?" It was the first Detective Walsh heard anything connecting Keegan's murder to Kildare—or, anyone else. "It's my understanding Keegan Sullivan was really nothing more than a drunk who was good at tying knots. And, from what I know of him? Not too far off the mark . . ."

Aidan nodded. "That's true—but, it would be just like Finn Kildare to stick someone on a trawler who could get information for him. You know—keeping his nose in my daughter's business."

"Someone easily bought . . ."

"Aye—and, that was Keegan Sullivan."

Again, Graham was quiet as he began to connect the dots. "So, just to make sure I'm understanding you correctly—you're saying, Aidan, Fin Kildare may be a suspect in your daughter's murder?" Another pause. "That's quite an accusation . . ."

Aidan could offer no more than a weak smile. "It's not an accusation, Graham. Just a broken-hearted man's thinking. And, of course, Kildare didn't know Smokey was already on my radar . . ." The aging fisherman didn't take his eyes from Detective Walsh. "I know as sure as I'm sittin' here, Smokey was keeping eyes on my daughter—and, I think Kildare knew it." He eyed Walsh. "So, why would Finn Kildare make it a point to bring up Smokey before I headed out fishing?"

"Well, I can only think of one thing . . ."

"Are we on the same page, Graham?"

A nod. "Classic deflection."

McNamara nodded. "I'm no detective, but that's sure as hell what it seems like to me!" Aidan sat forward in his chair, pointing his finger at Cobh's top detective. "I'm tellin' ya—Finn Kildare has something to do with it." A pause. "And, if he killed my daughter, he'll pay!"

Decklin Kilgarry sat at his kitchen table, the throwaway cell phone in front of him. Experience told him whoever beat the crap out of Miranda wouldn't wait long to call. *Whoever has the number*, he thought, staring at the phone, *needs me out of the way* . . . It made sense, too—if, in fact, Borja were in charge of a salmon poaching operation in Ireland, he'd want to take out whomever got in his way as quickly as possible.

As he sat, thoughts turned to the young woman who had the guts to issue a warning—a kindness certain to come to the attention of Carmine Borja. After her call, Decklin again enlisted the help of his U.S. colleague, finally divulging the depth of his unofficial investigation. "If we don't get a handle on this, Mason, someone else is going to die . . ."

Unfortunately, intel takes time.

Suddenly, the burner phone rang, yanking him from his thoughts. Quickly, he jotted down the caller's number, silently counting the number of rings—after seven, the call disconnected.

Wasting no time, Decklin texted the number to Mason, asking for a speedy reply and, within twenty, he had his answer. "Silvio Socorro—the number's from Barcelona."

Decklin chuckled. "I can't believe he was stupid enough to use his own cell! I hoped, though . . ."

"Do you want me to pull anything?"

Relieved he had someone on his side whom he could trust, somehow, it made things easier. "If you have time—

there's another name I'd like you check out, but all I have is a first name . . ."

"And, that is?"

"Miranda . . ." For the next few minutes, Decklin filled in the gaps. "If she has something to do with Borja, her name will probably show up somewhere . . ."

"Agreed—I'll get back with you." With that, Decklin's contact severed the connection.

We're getting close, he thought, again looking at the caller's number. *I hope it's not too late . . .*

Chapter 23

As it happened, Smokey Alvera turned up as a deckhand working on a new trawler, its captain unfamiliar to those who lived in the village. Aidan McNamara, however, recognized Alvera instantly, questioning whether he should keep an eye on him. Should he take care of business himself? Or, tip off Walsh their boy was back? I *don't have time to be bird-dogging anybody*, Aidan tried to convince himself as he readied his boat for the day's catch. Still, he had to admit, revenge would feel mighty good, even if it meant changing his life forever.

Filtered evening light allowed him to glance undetected every few minutes at the new trawler, noting its captain did nothing except bark orders at his deckhands.

"What an ass," Aidan muttered under his breath, knowing there wasn't a deckhand in Cobh who'd put up with such a thing. Yes, his daughter was known for a rough tongue, but, everyone knew she'd do anything to keep her deckhands safe.

It was then he decided.

Stepping into the small cabin, he closed the door—just in case someone came calling. Grabbing his cell from his pocket, he tapped the screen a few times, then connected. "Walsh? Aidan McNamara . . ."

Moments later, he clicked off, satisfied he did the right thing. Bracing himself against a strong offshore wind, again he stepped onto his deck. Then?

Dropped like a rock.

As far as Silvio Socorro was concerned, the disgusting Daft Irishman was an establishment for losers preferring to drink their fishing profits. So, when he decided to eavesdrop on gossip from those who lived and worked in the darkest corners of the fishing profession, it was only at the behest of his employer. Personally?

He wouldn't be caught dead in such a place.

Nodding to the barkeep, he scanned the dank, depressing room, catching Miranda's eye. Quickly, she turned from him, refusing to attract a reason to speak to her—and, he felt the same. In his mind, since their last encounter, she'd be stupid to make waves—especially since he reported back to Borja after securing the phone number written on a napkin.

Even so, it never hurt to make his presence known.

A pint finally in front of him, he turned on his barstool, watching every fishermen who opened the Daft's door. Then, precisely at midnight, its newest patron turned out to be the captain of the new trawler—obviously, an outsider.

A misfit.

Socorro watched as the captain spoke to the barkeep, then made his way to the back of the tavern, claiming a spot at a small, empty table. At first glance, there was something familiar about him, sparking an immediate feeling of distrust—clearly, the captain didn't exactly fit in with the Daft's clientele.

Then again, neither did he.

A little too classy, he thought. But, it wasn't until Decklin Kilgarry pulled on the Daft's door, a shiver coursed up Socorro's spine, as if suddenly confronted by a ghostly apparition.

Dressed like a seasoned fisherman and in keeping with his story to Miranda of bringing a new trawler to Cobh, he paused for a moment before heading to the bar. If she recognized him, she didn't let on, certain doing so would mean another unpleasant episode with Silvio Socorro.

Socorro watched as the man he didn't recognize sat at the end of the bar, slightly obscured, yet a perfect position for keeping a wary eye. Although usually not a man with an intuitive bent, there was something about him Socorro instantly didn't trust. Obviously, he was somebody attempting to blend in and act like nobody—the question was why.

Suddenly, without thinking, Socorro pulled his cell from his jacket pocket, tapped the screen, then waited. Watching.

Within seconds, Decklin Kilgarry felt the buzz of the throwaway cell in his pocket, yet resisted the urge to check its screen. *Interesting,* he thought as he sipped his beer, *nothing until I came here . . .*

A cop's intuition.

"I have no idea what hit me," Aidan claimed as he sat across from Detective Walsh for the third time. "When I stepped up to the deck, it was lights out . . ."

"When?"

"Yesterday evening—it didn't occur to me to look at the time. Day was done, though . . ."

"Any idea of who wanted you out of the way?" Graham tapped the end of his pen on his desk, irritated by the whole damned situation. "Any reason?"

"Nope—unless it were Kildare. He's as daft as they come—he only keeps a lid on when it best serves him. But, after the last time he was on my trawler?" A pause. "I doubt it . . ."

"Was anything missing?"

"Only my cell phone—why someone would want that, I have no idea. I barely know how to work the damned thing!"

And, there it was . . .

The connecting thread.

So, for the next twenty or so minutes, Detective Graham Walsh took Aidan McNamara's personal statement. To Walsh's thinking, the person who called Decklin Kilgarry's cell phone shortly after Miranda gave him the heads up and the one who kyped McNamara's cell were one and the same.

Socorro.

If there were one thing Silvio Socorro wasn't, it was stupid. After watching Decklin Kilgarry at the Daft, there was no doubt the wannabe fisherman was there for nefarious reasons—the only problem was he had no idea of his true identity.

No one did, Miranda included.

That meant digging deeper into Miranda's list of contacts—something that could wait until the following day. "I'll be on your doorstep tomorrow at ten," he whispered to her as he prepared to leave the Daft. "Don't disappoint me."

A nod to assure him she wouldn't, she watched as he was the last to leave.

But, disappoint him, she did.

When he pounded on her door the following morning? Split.

"There's enough here to get you to Dublin . . ." Decklin gently touched Miranda's bruised face. "I'm sorry I got you in trouble . . ."

"You didn't know . . ."

"No—I didn't. But, the least I can do is make sure you're safe. I made arrangements with a friend of mine, and you'll have a place to stay for as long as you need."

Miranda looked at him, her eyes filling with tears. "I don't know what to say . . ."

"Don't say anything—but, if you really want to help, I need to know your relationship with Smokey Alvera, Silvio Socorro, and Carmine Borja."

"They'll kill me, if they find out!"

"I promise you'll be safe—within a few weeks, you'll have a new identity, so they'll never find you."

"How . . ."

"It doesn't matter—but, after today, you and I will never speak again." Decklin paused, then a deep sigh. "The truth is, however, if you don't tell me what I need to know, Borja will never be brought to justice."

Miranda was silent for a few minutes, weighing the pros and cons. There was little doubt Carmine Borja would send Socorro to look for her once he learned she skipped out on her job at the Daft—and, him.

Suddenly, she straightened, looking Decklin in the eye. "I'll tell you everything I know . . ."

As much as Decklin wanted to hug her, he didn't—no sense in giving someone a reason to look. "Thank you . . ."

So, for the next two hours in a tiny, out-of-the-way restaurant, Miranda spilled her guts, determined to make Carmine Borja and Silvio Socorro pay for treating her like a piece of trash. When she walked out the door, leaving Decklin to process what she just told him?

He could've sworn she was walking a little bit straighter.

Two days later?

Silvio Socorro was found deader than a doornail on a Barcelona dock with two black roses crammed down his throat. A message?

Perhaps.

Chapter 24

Smokey Alvera approached the vintage trawler, hoping to find no one on board except for the captain. "Permission to come aboard," he called, then waited, jamming his hands in his pockets.

Aidan McNamara opened the cabin window, glaring at the man who dared ask permission to board his vessel. "What do you want?"

"I have information . . ."

"What kind of information?"

Smokey reached into his jacket pocket, extracting a pack of cigarettes. As if he had all the time in the world, he lit one, took a deep draw, then returned his attention to the captain. "It's about your daughter."

Recalling his recent conversation with Finn Kildare, Aidan McNamara couldn't help recognizing the irony—it certainly lent credence to his theory that Kildare was attempting to deflect suspicion away from himself. And, if that weren't his reason for throwing Smokey under the bus? It would behoove him to let the deckhand speak. "Come aboard!"

Moments later, Smokey stood in front of the seasoned fisherman, a slight smile on his lips. "I'm surprised we haven't met sooner," he commented, then took another prolonged drag.

"And, who might you be?"

A smirk. "Please, Captain—don't insult me. You know very well who I am. So, if you want information about who murdered your daughter . . ."

"Whose boat?"

Smokey thought for a moment, not quite understanding McNamara's request. "I . . . do you mean whose boat am I working on now?"

A nod. 'That's what I said—whose boat?"

Smokey turned, then pointed to a trawler several slips away. "It's new."

Aidan's eyes followed the pointing finger. "Who's the captain?"

Suddenly, Smokey's gut told him the impromptu visit wasn't the best idea. "Look, do you want to hear what I have to say, or not?"

"Not really. Now, get your ass off of my boat!"

Captain Joseph Varela sat back in his chair, not taking his eyes from the small screen. "Who's that," he asked, his Spanish accent thick with accusation.

"Aidan McNamara." Varela's right-hand man knew never to offer extemporaneous information unless asked.

"Why is Smokey pointing at us?"

"I have no idea, Sir—but, it appears he's divulging our location."

Both men watched as the Anna Marie's deckhand suddenly disembarked Aidan's trawler, then made his way back to his new boat, taking only a moment to crush his cigarette on the dock, then kick it into the water.

"He doesn't know of the cameras?"

"No, Sir—I had them installed before he reported for duty. They're small and nearly undetectable—unless you're looking for them."

"Excellent." Varela smirked, knowing if the opportunity presented itself, taking care of Smokey Alvera wouldn't be a problem. "I want to know everyone he talks to, and where he goes when he's not on the boat . . "

If there were a chance Borja's bottom-rung man were playing both sides?

A situation quickly rectified.

Eyes on the water from a seaside home, Miranda Byrne cycled through her time in Cobh—for the few years she was there, it turned out to be quite lucrative. Of course, no one suspected her responsibilities were two-fold and, as far as Decklin Kilgarry was concerned?

A happy accident.

It was touching, she thought as she swiped her sunglasses with the fabric of her skirt, then held them up to the sun to make certain the smudge was gone. *Unfortunately, he isn't as bright as he thinks he is . . .*

"My dear! How nice to see you again!" Carmine Borja's booming voice carried off the veranda, causing one of his caretakers to look up. "It has been a long time, yes?" He took her hand, kissed it, then gestured to his housekeeper to bring drinks.

"It feels good to be away from the stench of fish . . ."

"Yes—but, your time there was worth it. And, for what it's worth, you have my apology. Silvio enjoyed his job a little too much, I'm afraid."

"He didn't know?"

"That you were directing operations?" A pause. "No— no one knows. A secret to be enjoyed only by a chosen few, don't you agree?"

Miranda smiled, enjoying the fact her instructions were carried out as planned—most of them, anyway. Shifting her focus from the sea to him, it was clear she had items to discuss. "The fact is there's a concerted effort to shut us down in Ireland, as you know—and, they're getting close."

Borja nodded, knowing he was in for a tongue lashing. "There have been complications," he admitted, hoping to persuade her they were unavoidable circumstances.

"Three dead? Those unavoidable circumstances?" She waited, a familiar irritation beginning to rise. "I thought my instructions were to speak to me first, and I was to be the only one making decisions!"

"I thought . . ."

A dismissive wave. "I don't want to hear about what you thought! Now, because of your stupidity, we have a cop from the States with a magnifying glass on us!"

"How do you . . ."

Miranda accepted a drink from the housekeeper, then waited until she returned to her station. "How I know is none of your business—but, Carmine, I think you have a bit of a mess to clean up, don't you?"

"We have a trawler in Cobh—but, I must be honest. With three people dead in such a small area, it may be best to fly under the radar this season."

"Are you suggesting we pull our operations, and lose millions?"

"Well, there are people who will stop at nothing . . ."

Miranda was silent for a few moments, aware the Cobh operation was in jeopardy. "With Delgado gone, who do we have watching out for our interests?"

"Joseph and his crew—and, Smokey."

"That's it? I certainly hope you're not counting on Smokey Alvera for anything!" A pause. "So, what you're saying is we have no one to infiltrate other trawlers—is that correct?"

Borja said nothing, obviously growing weary of his boss's insinuations. "There's nothing to lead them to us . . ."

"With three murders on their hands?" Suddenly, Miranda stood, then drained her glass. "Is there anyone left whom you trust—at least a little?"

"Only Silvio . . ."

"Silvio's dead, you fool! You didn't expect me to take what he dished out, did you?"

"But, he didn't . . ."

Miranda smiled. "That may be—but, for my taste, Carmine? He enjoyed his work a little too much, and we can't take the chance of drawing any more attention to ourselves." She paused, carefully weighing her next move. "Leave me—do nothing until you hear my voice."

Borja stood, humiliation apparent. "As you wish . . ."

"Exactly. As I wish . . ."

Although it took a few days, Detective Walsh caught wind of Smokey Alvera's visit to Aidan's trawler, sparking more interest in the young Spaniard. "We know he's involved in the poaching ring," he commented to Decklin and the O'Quinns on his day off. "We just don't know to what extent."

"Well, do you want to know what I think," Alannah interjected, her words silencing everyone at the kitchen table.

"Of course," Decklin grinned. "You're as much a part of this think tank as any of us . . ."

"Okay—well, it occurs to me it would be difficult to get a foothold in a town as small as Cobh."

"Meaning?"

Alannah focused on her cousin. "Doesn't it make sense to convince someone who already lives here to join the salmon poaching cause?"

"You mean a traitor," her husband asked, not liking the idea of someone duplicitous among them. "Why would one of us do such a thing?"

"Money . . ." Decklin nodded to Alannah. "Go on . . ."

"Exactly. You know money talks, and I think it spoke loudly enough to someone who didn't have any problem throwing us under the bus."

"But, who?" Connor glanced at Decklin then back at his wife. "Do you have someone in mind?"

"Well—not really. But, it makes sense, don't you think?"

Detective Walsh agreed. "It does—but, we suspected Dominic Delgado was calling the shots for someone higher up the ladder."

"I know—Borja. And, I agree with you—all I'm saying is I feel there's someone else involved. Someone we know nothing about—and, what better way to conceal it than having a traitor among us?"

Decklin, Walsh, and Connor had to admit she had a point, and it was a theory they hadn't entertained. "Okay," Walsh commented, "Let's start making a list . . ."

Standing just beyond the perimeter of the O'Quinn's property, there was little doubt one of Cobh's finest was spending a little too much time with two of the village's longtime locals—and, it wasn't the first time. *Gettin' a little too cozy, if ya ask me*, he thought as he stepped further back into the shadows just in case. But, what bothered him most?

He was the topic of conversation.

Of course, there was no way he could truly know what was being said as he peered through the kitchen window from a distance. Street sense, however, cued him to exactly what he needed to know, and it was becoming all too clear a shakeup was in the offing. If he weren't careful, all eyes would certainly land on him, ruining everything, and that was simply a chance he couldn't take.

As shadows deepened, he took one final look, then pulled his cell phone from his jacket pocket. To be extra careful, he turned his back to the O'Quinn window to block the illuminating screen—then, a tap. "We have a problem," he informed his contact.

"Then, do something about it."

"I'm afraid it's not going to be that easy . . ." Suddenly, he turned, again facing the seaside cottage, watching as Detective Graham Walsh bid goodbye to his hosts, then spoke a few private words to Decklin Kilgarry on the cottage porch. "I'll await orders . . ."

Connection severed.

Moments later, he circled through the trees, away from prying eyes and it was there, in Ireland's moonlight, he made the most important decision of his life.

A right decision.

It had been a long time since Finn Kildare had reason to pat himself on the back. For the first time in years, he landed on fishing grounds yielding the best salmon of his career, and the pleasure of a little extra jingle in his pocket was something to savor. A renewed respect, of sorts—if not from others, then for himself. The truth was he had few friends, most abandoning him shortly after high school when his mates decided he was no longer cool. Only a liability.

But, he didn't care.

Going it alone became a way of life staying with him for decades—and, though he never had the pleasure of having a beautiful woman on his arm, things in that department were about to change. In fact, that was why he decided to take matters into his own hands when it came to making changes in his life. Aging, he realized, wasn't all it was cracked up to be and, if truth be told, he was a bit lonely. But, if anyone asked? He kept salient points of his personal life to himself—what he did was nobody's damned business.

Of course, there was work to be done, but, when said and done, he'd have a life of which he could only dream, and it was his for the taking if everything went according to plan. What wasn't going according to plan, however, was Decklin Kilgarry showing up unwanted and unannounced. When first appearing in town, there was an air about Kilgarry Finn didn't like, although Kildare never considered him a threat in any way.

Until Keegan Sullivan downed his final drink.

An unfortunate necessity, Kildare convinced himself—but, the truth was Cobh's town drunk was nothing more than a patsy, and a damned good one. With more than a few synapses fried over his lifetime, Sullivan had little to yield when it came to results—but, what he did have was allegiance. Furious about the salmon poaching situation, more than a few times he bellowed in the bar about how everyone was getting screwed—and, if he had anything to say about it, someone would pay. What Keegan Sullivan didn't know?

His words were a definitive threat.

Finn chuckled, recalling how easy it was to point Sullivan in any direction, knowing he'd arrive at his destination eventually. Some in the village refused to admit his lack of worth to their community, giving him the benefit of the doubt whenever he seemed to need it—which was often. Still, captains of trawlers—as much as they hated the thought of hiring him—knew Keegan's salt as a sailor was in his ability to keep operations moving smoothly, especially when Wingo McNamara was at the trawler's helm. *Everyone knew she was the worst captain*, he thought, again chuckling, totally delighted with his own ability to carry out orders better than anyone he knew.

Especially his own.

Although, if Kildare were to be completely honest, taking orders from someone else grated on his last nerve—a situation he'd choose to rectify when things were a tad more solidified. Still, as much as it went against his upbringing, he chose to remain mum, allowing orchestration of his plan to play out. *It's wiser that way*, he thought as he studied a ripped calendar on his workroom wall. But, was it?

Perhaps.

Suddenly, his mind flipped to Decklin Kilgarry, a familiar anger beginning to rise. When Kilgarry first landed in the village, there was little to think. Little to analyze. But, when doing a bit of research of his own after their first meeting at Connor O'Quinn's?

Well, let's just say history has a way of repeating itself.

Chapter 25

Decklin switched on the light, dimming it slightly before making himself comfortable in what quickly became his favorite chair shortly after moving into the cottage. Promising himself he wasn't going to budge until he had something to show for his efforts, he flipped his legal pad to a blank page, then clicked his pen.

Alannah's comment about a traitor among them struck him as a possibility, inviting a more targeted inspection of those in Cobh who may prefer to fly under the radar. First on his list?

Smokey Alvera.

At first convinced Alvera was nothing more than a two-bit player in a larger operation, it was a possible waste of time to go through his list of reasons to consider Alvera a suspect. Even so, experience told Decklin never to rule out those with a lengthy rap sheet even if the crime doesn't match. Although Alvera appeared to be someone without clout, based on what Decklin and Graham uncovered so far, there was little doubt he played a more important role than originally thought.

Drawing a line down the center of his legal pad, it was the typical pros and cons thing—from the time he was wet behind the ears and when it came to investigations, he included a horizontal line two-thirds down. Quickly, he labeled each block—top suspects, who has what to gain, and who's the boss. More than once during his career he learned the person running the show was often the one sitting on the sidelines, watching, completely insulated from suspicion.

So, there he sat with a legal pad on his lap, a shot of Irish whiskey at the ready should he need it—and, by the time the rising sun glinted on the sea's surface, Decklin Kilgarry turned their case in a direction no one anticipated.

Including himself.

When it comes to murder, one thing is certain—it's pretty black and white. Get caught, or don't—and, so far, not getting caught was winning. Yet, with no legal standing in the country let alone the Cobh community, his hands were tied.

Knowing he should include Graham in his plans, intuition's nudge cued him otherwise—and, as much as Decklin wanted to convince himself leaving Detective Walsh in the dark was for his own good, it simply wasn't true.

Decklin simply didn't want him in the way.

Four hours after his all-nighter thinking about Cobh's murders?

On a flight to Spain.

"Your friend from the States just headed to Dublin airport..."

"And?" Miranda Byrne leaned closer to the vanity's mirror, then stepped back for a more scrutinizing assessment.

"And, what? I just thought you'd want to know—I happened to pass him on the road, and curiosity got the better of me."

"You tailed him?"

"Aye—to the train station. It wasn't too hard to figure out he was on his way to the Dublin Airport." A pause. "A flight to where is what I want to know..."

"With any luck, he's going back where he belongs." Miranda turned for a side view.

"I doubt it—my gut tells me he's on to something."

Finally, she sat, allowing her Cobh contact her full attention. "And, just what do you think that is?"

"You."

For the first time in the conversation, Miranda listened carefully. "I don't think so—he knows nothing about me other than my time at the Daft."

At least, that's what she wanted Finn Kildare to believe—if everything went according to plan, it wouldn't make a bit of difference because she'd be long gone.

Untraceable.

"That's all well and good, but, you know as well as I, there's a reason he's still sniffing around Cobh—and, I think it's because of the murders. He's a cop—justice runs deep in his veins, and his blood pulses with a need to set the record straight. It's what he does, Miranda—it's an insatiable drive."

Miranda listened, slightly stunned at Kildare's ability to turn a phrase. "Well—I appreciate your concern. However, Decklin Kilgarry is no longer my concern . . ."

As tempting as it was to stay at a quaint, Spanish hotel was, Decklin opted for something a little more out of the way and in need of repair—somewhere he could come and go without curious eyes.

First things first, however.

Not bothering to unpack, a call to Mason was first priority since his quick departure from Cobh didn't allow for a private call. After a brief conversation and within the hour,

Decklin had everything he needed to know about Miranda Byrne. *Well, now . . .* he thought as he read through her dossier. *What a tangled web we weave . . .*

Committing certain information to memory, he grabbed his coat, then patted his shirt pocket to make certain he had his phone. Although carrying it posed a calculable risk, it would be foolish to be without a way to contact authorities—or, Walsh, if needed.

The over-the-water flight allowed time needed to draft a plan, surveillance first on the list and, within the hour, he sat outside of Miranda Byrne's estate, careful to remain out of sight from numerous camera lenses. "A lot more than one," he muttered as he counted multiple surveillance cameras mounted not only at the gate, but on the front of her palatial estate, as well. *This is going to be a lot more difficult than I thought . . .*

"Have you seen your cousin around," Graham asked as Alannah poured him a cup of tea.

"You mean this isn't a social visit," she laughed.

"I'm afraid not—although, I wish it were!"

Connor grinned, realizing the good detective was there on specific business. "Obviously, there's a reason you're here—and, I'm guessing it has to do with our case."

Graham was quiet for a moment, considering how much he should divulge—but, since Connor and his wife had been in on his investigation from the beginning, what harm could it do? "It does—and, I'm thinking Decklin may be able to give me a hand." Another pause. "Do you have any idea where I can find him?"

Alannah shook her head. "I haven't seen him for a couple of days," she confided. "It's not like him . . ."

So, for the next few minutes, Detective Walsh sipped tea with his favorite Cobh residents, his mind never giving up the idea the D.C. detective was up to something. With that in mind, it seemed prudent to check travel manifests just in case.

You know—a cop's gut.

Miranda's tone didn't exactly sit well with the Irish fisherman, nor did her dismissal of what he considered possible critical information. As far as he was concerned, she was a bit too cavalier when it came to maintaining her own business. Arrogance?

Of course,

Still, his concern didn't abate as he watched the setting sun across the water, the knowledge she was using him ever-present. If he would've thought about it?

Obvious.

But, desperation does funny things to a man—to anyone—and, all he cared about was how he could free his village from her grip. There was always the possibility she would do something stupid, but he doubted it. If she did?

Her entire organization would be history.

The more he thought about it, the more an unsettling agitation took root—a feeling all too familiar. The fact he opened up to Miranda Byrne a little more than he planned was a mistake, and as he considered the consequences?

Not good.

There was no doubt Miranda was a woman who'd use any weakness to her advantage, and anything Finn Kildare said or did would be perfect fodder.

It was then he decided to take matters into his own hands. *I'll find Kilgarry,* he promised himself, tapping his cell to life so he could check rail times to Dublin.

He needs to know . . .

Chapter 26

Decklin shifted his weight in the rental car, the injury from when he took a bullet as a rookie making sitting in the cramped vehicle more than uncomfortable. Even so, it wasn't something he hadn't endured before, convincing him the pain was worth it.

And, apparently, it was . . .

Shortly before two o'clock, a familiar black sedan pulled up in front of the gate, its driver clearly familiar with the access process. Deftly, he punched in a few numbers, waiting as it opened slowly, and, as Decklin watched through the binos, there was no mistaking the vehicle.

Borja!

Graham Walsh nodded to the flight attendant as he disembarked, his mind squarely on what he needed to accomplish. After learning Alannah hadn't seen her cousin for a few days, something didn't sit well with him, and it wasn't difficult to figure out Kilgarry was off on his own. A quick check of the customer manifests for the rail station as well as the Dublin Airport revealed he traveled to Barcelona with no return date.

The question was why?

Of course, he knew the answer instantly when he learned of Decklin's destination—and, it was an answer he didn't want to consider. Even with knowing his U.S. counterpart's skill and experience, doing business in Europe was a completely different thing. Should he have the pleasure of encountering Carmine Borja or one of his men, reaction would be fierce—and, most likely, fatal.

Stepping into the Barcelona sun, hair on the back of his neck stood at attention, a shudder coursing his spine.

A portend?

Undeniably.

"You're looking lovely today, my dear . . ." Carmine Borja smiled as he kissed Miranda's hand. "I assume you must have something important to discuss . . ."

"Indeed." Launching a scathing glare, she gestured to a chair not far from her, but far enough. "Sit."

He did, without comment.

"I received a call from our Cobh operative . . ."

Borja smiled. "Kildare?"

A nod.

"Well, it's interesting you refer to him as an 'operative'—a wannabe is more like it." Another smile. "But, I'm quite certain you didn't summon me to discuss my thoughts about Mr. Kildare . . ."

"Your thoughts about anything are neither here nor there . . ." Miranda paused, thinking of what she must do next. "According to Kildare, Decklin Kilgarry landed in Barcelona today . . ."

"Kilgarry's here?"

"I believe that's what I just said."

Borja concentrated on his shoes, anger seething. It was uncustomary for anyone to get under his skin, but, for some reason, the whole Cobh operation created a pit in his stomach.

"Well?"

Carmine Borja slowly lifted his gaze, parking it directly on the woman in front of him. "I don't like the sound of it . . ."

"Neither do I—but, we must protect my assets no matter the circumstances."

"Don't you mean our assets?"

A smirk. "Same thing, don't you think?" A pause. "Either way, I believe it's time to allow things to cool down . . ."

It was all Borja could do not to snort with disgust—especially since he previously suggested that particular tactic.

"So, I believe it's time for me to . . ." Again, she paused, noticing the look on Borja's face. "Is there something you wish to say, Carmine?"

"Of course not—please continue."

A brief silence. "As I was saying, I believe it's time for me to take a bit of a sabbatical . . ."

There was, naturally, no disguising her true intent of removing herself from the investigative limelight—out of sight, out of mind seemed a much more intelligent approach to her current dilemma than hanging around waiting for the worst. "Perhaps, it's best," Carmine agreed. "Where will you be in case I need . . ."

"I doubt you'll need me—you're quite capable of handling things on your own." Allowing her gaze to linger on him for a few moments longer than usual, it was clear she was throwing Carmine Borja under the bus. *Business is business*, she thought, as she considered the best manner in which to effect her disappearance.

What did Carmine think?

Miranda's being out of the picture was good news.

The truth was Miranda Byrne was beginning to get on his nerves, and he didn't care for her recent tactics. Allowing the Washington D.C. cop to get too close was evidence of that, indicating it may be time to effect a corporate takeover. An idea he toyed with over the last several months, protecting his own ass became an all-too-familiar thought. "If trouble heads your way?"

"Meaning Kilgarry?"

"Or, anyone else—if things take a turn and you need to know about it, don't you think it's wise for me to warn you?"

Miranda was quiet for a moment, instinctively knowing he was right. "Alright—I see your point." A pause. "I'll be on the coast."

"Ours?"

She shook her head. "No—Cobh. It's in my best interest to keep an eye on things . . ."

"You think that's wise?"

A glare. "If I didn't think it were wise, I wouldn't be doing it, would I?" Without realizing it, she pursed her lips and frowned, leaving a distasteful scowl dipping into Carmine's memory. "No one knows of the cottage . . ."

"Locals do."

"Well, I can't be worried about such a thing—it's far enough out of sight, and no one will give it a second thought. Besides, this time of year, it's always shrouded in mist, so no one will come snooping."

Borja was silent for a few moments, quickly figuring out his best plan. "Then, I shall leave you to it—I'll be in touch if I hear anything." Suddenly, he stood, discontent on display—it was then he recognized Miranda Byrne no longer held the trump card.

He did.

After Borja departed, it was clear there would be little action until the following day, prompting him to wrap up his surveillance. As he placed the binos in their case, however, he couldn't help feeling he wasn't alone. Quickly, he scanned the area, nothing appearing out of place—even so, as he pulled away, a reflection in his rearview caught his attention—one he hadn't noticed earlier.

He'd be lying if he said his heart weren't racing as he made his way down the curved hillside. If one of Miranda's security guys caught the license plate?

He wouldn't be hard to trace.

"I appreciate your time," Detective Walsh commented, extending his hand. "I know it's valuable . . ."

"What can I do for you?" Detective Javier Simonetta

flashed even, pearly whites rivaling Decklin Kilgarry's. "It's not every day I have an Irishman sitting in front of me . . ."

So, for the next thirty minutes, Graham Walsh filled in his Spanish counterpart on everything, leaving nothing to conjecture. "I know he's here . . ."

Simonetta sat back in his chair, fingertips gently stroking a slightly scraggly, greying Van Dyke beard. "He well may be," he finally agreed, knowing a cop worth his weight would follow any lead. "Carmine Borja has been on our radar for years, but, I'm embarrassed to admit the name Miranda Byrne is new."

"I'm not surprised—from what Kilgarry and I can figure, she's been running the show for the last five years, but on the down-low. At least, in Cobh—my guess is she's international, including Canada. Maybe the States . . ."

"Aliases?"

"Maybe. If so, we don't know them . . ."

Both men were quiet for a few moments, each trying to figure out the best approach. "I'll put a tail on Borja," he finally agreed. "Do you know where Byrne is?"

Walsh shook his head. "No—but, I'm willing to bet Kilgarry does. Find him, and we find our targets . . ."

Simonetta nodded. "I'll locate Kilgarry, too. Keep your phone handy . . ."

After spending the following day surveilling Miranda Byrne's villa with nothing to show for his efforts, Decklin began to assume the worst. *No one in, and no one out*, he thought as he glanced in his rearview mirror. *If she's gone*, he considered as he turned left onto a narrow street taking him toward the city, *there's really no reason to be here . . .* Unless, of course, he felt like taking on Carmine Borja by himself.

Perhaps not the smartest idea.

Then again, no one ever said I was smart . . .

It's an interesting moment when a man declares himself guilty of something, yet refuses to acknowledge underlying causes for such a disquieting, personal proclamation. It requires a special sort of responsibility, something often taking a header when confronted with emotional needs.

Finnian Kildare, III was no different.

As he pondered his partnership with a woman clearly beyond his reach, he couldn't help but grant himself penance for his actions. *I did what I had to do to save our industry*, he again convinced himself, well aware his reasons didn't exactly line up with what the lovely Miranda expected of him. *Someone had to do something . . .*

Indeed.

Little did he suspect, however, the stench of corruption would take him to a place in his life forcing understanding of his ancestors. Subterfuge, he discovered from family legend, was inborn and, as with those before him, weaving a story for the masses to believe was easy. A gift, of sorts—at least, that's what he preferred to call it.

In the beginning, nearly five years prior and when Miranda Byrne landed in Cobh for the first time, it didn't take a genius to figure out she was out of place. *Something about her just didn't quite fit*, he thought, recalling the first time he noticed her at the Daft. It wasn't that she was a woman of class because she wasn't—but, there was something about her he couldn't quite figure out. And, when she set her sights on him?

Something was up.

Others thought so, too—Keegan Sullivan and Wingo McNamara most notable—and, when salmon began to noticeably decline, it wasn't too difficult to figure out someone was wedging dissension into Cobh's fishing industry.

But, as so often happens, winnowing the village's population through attrition became a way of life, and it wasn't until declining circumstances were no longer tolerable did locals begin to understand the consequences of accepting someone new into their community. Although greenhorns were always welcomed in the past, new faces began to snag suspicion from trawler captains, but there was little they could do—they needed hands, and whomever they belonged to made no difference.

It was a situation bringing in more money than Miranda Byrne could count, greed prompting her to continue operations in spite of increasing risk. But, it wasn't until Keegan Sullivan began raising raucous objection, however, did she have an inkling of who could potentially cause problems. She didn't appreciate anyone's mouth, particularly when it belonged to someone who had the brain of a gnat—exactly what she thought of the drunk Irishman.

A gross miscalculation.

Finn Kildare knew differently, however, so when Keegan's body was discovered bobbing perilously against the piers, there was little doubt in his mind the fisherman met his end by the hands of a traitor among them.

Still, it wasn't up to him to make waves—which is why, he supposed, he chose to deflect all suspicion from him, should there be any. Asking Keegan to work for him during the last fishing season was a stroke of genius, but, unfortunately, it didn't exactly work out as planned—especially for Sullivan. Still, there was information to be gleaned from his untimely passing and, as Finn recounted the past year's events, there was little doubt that with a bit of luck, Miranda Byrne's empire would topple.

It's time . . .

Decklin sat at the small desk in his hotel room, laptop open, its screen illuminating small lines etching his face, particularly around his eyes. It had been a long time since he experienced the frustrations of an investigation gone wrong, and it was something he refused to admit. *If Borja is here—and, I know he is—it's going to take more than me to bring him down . . .*

Just then, a strong, impatient rap on his door.

Of course, his first inclination was to remain silent, knowing no one knew of his trip, let along his location. Still, something prompted him to cross to the door and peer through the peephole. "Damn it, Walsh!" As much as he didn't want to, he opened the door with a grin. "What the hell are you doing here?"

Shaking hands as Decklin closed the door, Walsh eyed the sparse furnishings. "Going minimal, I see . . ."

"More incognito, don't you think?" Then, a serious question as Decklin invited the Irishman to take a seat in the only chair. "Again, my friend—what are you doing here?"

"In my line of work, Kilgarry, it's customary to inform your partner of impromptu trips to apprehend a criminal." A pause. "That's why you're here, isn't it? To bring Miranda Byrne to justice?"

Decklin said nothing, impressed by his Irish counterpart. "Was I that transparent?"

"Not really—it's just that I know you better than you may suspect!"

"Unfortunately, I have nothing to show . . ."

So, for the next couple of hours, Detectives Kilgarry and Walsh compared notes, Graham listening intently to Decklin's plan to bring salmon poaching in his village to its knees. "Miranda Byrne is the brains—which leaves Carmine Borja to pick up the pieces."

"Pieces?"

"Well, kind of—after spending the day surveilling her villa today, it's clear she's no longer there." He paused. "It feels empty . . ."

"Any idea of where she might've gone?"

"Maybe—but, as long as we have Carmine Borja in our sights, perhaps it's time to pay him a visit."

"Without backup?"

Decklin grinned. "If I know you, Walsh, you paid a visit to the local authorities before knocking on my door—how else would you have located me so fast?"

"Guilty as charged."

"So, what do you think? Should we pay Mr. Borja a friendly visit?"

Walsh matched his grin with one of his own. "You have to ask?"

Chapter 27

*J*avier Simonetta eyed Decklin and Walsh in the rearview mirror. "I hope you realize," he commented, his tone in accordance with the seriousness of their destination, "your participation today is highly irregular . . ."

Decklin nodded. "We appreciate it—we also know you're as eager as we are to apprehend Borja." He paused, considering the confines of their upcoming interview—predicated on, of course, whether Borja were on his estate premises. Gaining access would be no problem—it was the gate guard Decklin worried about. "As soon as the gatekeeper knows we're on the premises, it won't be long until Borja goes underground . . ."

"He'll run," Walsh commented. "No doubt . . ."

"Perhaps, except they won't want to be involved." Simonetti paused. "We must be certain to work with our laws . . ."

Decklin glanced at Walsh, then focused again on the Spanish detective. "I'd love to ask a few questions—is that permissible?"

Detective Simonetta said nothing, understanding possible consequences. "No—I must interrogate, and to do otherwise will place our case in an untenable position." A glance. "I'm sure you understand . . ."

"There's been so much pain in our little village . . ."

Walsh smiled, enjoying hearing his U.S. partner refer to Cobh as home. "Indeed, there has," he agreed. Apprehending Borja will go a long way to bringing Miranda Byrne to justice."

Within fifteen, Simonetta pulled up to the villa's massive, custom-designed gate. "Ten bucks says we get in on the first try," Decklin said with a grin as he watched the gatekeeper shuffle toward them.

Simonetta and Walsh chuckled, although Simonetta figured there wouldn't be an issue. Lowering his window, he offered the middle-aged guard his friendliest smile. "Good morning!" A brief pause to quickly assess if it worked.

It didn't.

"We're here to see Carmine . . ." Simonetta glanced at his watch. "And, I'm late . . ."

The man eyed him, then leaned down and slightly closer to get a good look at the man in the passenger's seat. Then, he straightened, glancing back at the villa. "You're not on my list," the gatekeeper informed the Spanish detective in his native tongue.

Time for a little incentive. "Am I on your list now?"

The guard squinted as he peered at Detective Simonetta's identification—then, without comment, returned to his tiny gatehouse. "Understood."

With that, Javier slowly maneuvered the sedan through the gate, then headed toward the villa. "It's not as big as I thought," Decklin commented as Walsh kept watch for unwelcoming staff—and, cameras. "Eyes everywhere . . ."

Simonetta nodded. "Carmine Borja has much to protect."

"Front entrance?"

"Of course . . ."

Again, Decklin quickly scanned the surrounding area. "I trust you have appropriate documentation—no disrespect intended. I just want to be sure everything goes according to plan . . ."

Perhaps on a different day, Javier Simonetta would've taken the comment as an insult—that morning?

Nothing mattered except taking down Carmine Borja.

"I know I shouldn't be contacting you . . ." A pause. "But, I think you should know . . ."

"Know what," Carmine asked, irritation obvious.

"Well—although I hate to say, it appears Ms. Byrne isn't making the best decisions right now." Finnian Kildare, III, hesitated, hoping to read Borja's reaction even though he couldn't see him.

Silence.

"Decklin Kilgarry is in Barcelona as we speak," he continued, "yet, she appears unconcerned." Another pause. "I assume you know of him . . ."

Of course, it was against the organization's policy to contact those at the top no matter the circumstances—but, as Kildare spoke, Carmine couldn't help but consider how the Irish fisherman could be of assistance. "I hope you considered the consequences before contacting me," he commented, his words meant only for effect.

"I did—and, I would do it again, Sir." Calling Borja 'Sir' was enough to make Finn puke, but he was willing to do anything to save his village.

"You have three minutes . . ."

"I'll only need two, Sir . . ."

As anticipated, members of Borja's staff had little time to react. "Carmine Borja," Simonetta commanded, holding his identification in front of the housekeeper who opened the door.

Stepping aside and without a word, she allowed them to enter, then pointed to a winding staircase. "There," she directed in Spanish.

Now, had it been Decklin's investigation? A quiet ascent up the stairs for the thrill of surprise. Simonetta?

Not so much.

The Spaniard in the lead and with no effort toward silence, the three detectives climbed the stairs, each man listening to muffled conversation as they approached the top step. Simonetta pointed, then directed Decklin and Walsh to each side of the doorway at the end of the generous hallway. "Carmine Borja," he suddenly bellowed as he entered the room, identification in hand.

"Who the hell are you," Borja demanded, crossing to his desk while disconnecting his caller. "How did you get in here?"

"I suggest you keep your hands above the desk," Simonetta warned. "In fact, you may want to sit down," he suggested, pointing to a chair. "We have much to discuss . . ."

"I have nothing . . ."

"Sit down!"

Stunned, Borja sat. "My men will be here in moments," he declared, glancing at the doorway.

No one.

"Seriously? I guarantee your staff wants to stay as far away from you as possible . . ." A pause. "So, Carmine, it's time we had a little chat."

Borja snorted, the thrill of confrontation beginning to stir. "I'll tell you nothing."

Simonetta glanced at Walsh. "Will you close the door, please? And, lock it . . ."

With a nod, Graham complied, never taking his eyes from the squatty, well-dressed man sitting in a spindly chair meant only for design.

"I've always been a fair man," Javier began, "so, if you think it's wise to tell me what you know, I'll make sure your cooperation is taken into consideration. If not?" A pause. "Well, it's comforting, I suppose, to know where you'll be spending the rest of your days . . ."

Borja squirmed slightly, Javier Simonetta's words hitting their mark. An obvious finality about them, Borja began to wonder if, in fact, it would be in his best interest to cut a deal. "I'm listening . . ."

The beginning of the end?

With luck.

As much as she enjoyed her time in Cobh simply because of the fortune she was making, when Miranda Byrne pushed open the door to the cottage, there was nothing she hated more. If everything had gone according to plan, there would be no need to spend time in such a dank, God-forsaken place just to have time to get her head together to plan the best way to get out of Dodge.

Only after taking appropriate steps, however.

In her mind, she was guilty of nothing. Well, except the unfortunate demise of Silvio Socorro—and Keegan Sullivan, Wingo McNamara, and Dominic Delgado. But, since no one knew that little tidbit except Carmine, she was in the clear. Still—there was reason for concern, driving her to take matters into her own hands. With no one aware of her presence, it allowed an opportunity to observe from afar— and, those whom she suspected weren't pulling their weight within her organization?

Dealt with—swiftly and fiercely.

I've been in worse, she thought as she closed and locked the door, mentally patting herself on the back for her foresight to buy the cottage sight unseen when it came up for sale a few years back.

A wet, deep stench within the logs greeted her as she went from room to room—tiny as they were—its chill prompting her to glance at the wood-burning stove. *Exactly what I expected*, she thought, silently thanking her father for teaching her the ways of survival. "You never know when you'll need to save yourself," he advised as he taught her how to make a fire from Cheetos and a match.

Indeed.

"Tell me about the poaching operation . . ."

Carmine's jaw set. "I don't know what you're talking about . . ."

Casually, Simonetta pulled up an antique chair. "Come now, Carmine—you've been on our radar for quite some time, and it was only a matter of time."

Silence.

Suddenly, Javier rose, placing the chair in it's original position. "Okay—I tried. I'll tell my men we're on the way down . . ."

A lie, of course.

Within the few seconds it took Detective Simonetta to pull his cell from his pocket, Borja's common sense somehow managed to prevail. "I'm not at the top," he commented. "Not even close . . ."

Again, Detective Simonetta placed the small chair across from the man who seemed to be sweating considerably more than he was only moments prior. "Who is?"

An uncomfortable silence.

"Perhaps, you didn't hear me correctly—who calls the shots, Mr. Borja?" Common courtesy was always a plus.

Another silence, but only momentary. "Miranda Byrne."

Simonetta scanned the room, noticing a small wet bar. "Is there water in that refrigerator?"

Borja looked at him as if he were out of his mind, but nodded anyway.

"I hope you don't mind if we help ourselves—I have a feeling this will take a while." With that, Simonetta crossed to the small refrigerator, grabbed four bottles of water, then returned to his chair. "This is for you," he offered, handing one to Borja, then to Decklin and Walsh.

As odd as it was, there was something comforting in the detective's gesture—as it was designed to be. It also corroborated who was in charge. "Now," he continued, "tell me about Miranda Byrne . . ."

Suddenly disconnected from his call, there was little doubt in Finn Kildare's mind something was up, although—according the Miranda—Borja was intentionally rude. Even though Kildare never met him personally, it seemed odd to disconnect without securing the salient points of their conversation. Trouble?

Undoubtedly.

With such a thought on his mind, it took Finn a few moments to recall what no one else knew—Miranda Byrne had a little place outside of Cobh where few would care to visit. *Perfect for what she needs*, he thought, grabbing his backpack from the back of his workroom door. And, though he wasn't quite sure where her new living quarters were, as a life-time local, it shouldn't be too difficult to locate.

Checking it out was something he knew he needed to do, but the thought of confronting the woman who showed him a bit of attention was a meeting he didn't relish. Even though he played her as much as she played him? He'd be lying if he said her touch didn't make him feel something elusive for many years.

Within ten, he slipped out of town, his old work truck familiar to everyone in the village—a risk to be sure. But, as day tipped into evening, cottages and village homes were buttoned up, residents ready to relax after what were busy days.

By the time he reached the deserted road leading to Miranda's cabin, there was no one in sight, his heart beginning to pick up the pace. If, she were, in fact, there, it seemed more propitious to stand down rather than go in with guns blazing—figuratively, of course. By doing so, he had time to address the situation from a scant stand of trees across the road, then determine the best course of action.

With much resting in his hands, Finn Kildare made certain he had Graham Walsh's cell number on speed dial just in case. Although Finn hadn't briefed Walsh on his involvement trying to disrupt the poaching operation from within the ranks, Kildare knew the detective was smart enough to listen.

Especially when Finn had quite a story to tell.

"Miranda Byrne," Borja began with a certain distaste in his mouth, "*is* our operation."

"Meaning?"

"She runs everything, including who does what, when, and how—and, as one in her employ for considerable time, I can speak to her propensity to pay well . . ." Carmine paused, scanning his well-appointed, palatial office. "How else would I have achieved this?"

A rhetorical question.

"Go on. So, Miranda Byrne is the big gun . . ."

"It doesn't get any bigger—but, I suppose that's understandable, knowing her lineage. Then again, she's nothing but a greedy, cold-hearted woman—so, that helps."

Change of topic. "Who's idea was it to poach salmon?"

"Hers."

"Who was responsible for implementing the operation?"

"Miranda."

"Was there anyone else involved?"

Borja shook his head. "No—she took her time when placing key personnel in critical positions. If she couldn't find the right person to do her bidding, she wasn't one to make a rash decision." He paused, thinking of his own time within the organization—time, he wished he could take back.

"How did she find you?"

"It's no secret, Detective—unless you hail from different climes—my family was one of self-indulgence, self-satisfaction, and self-importance. For years, they ruled an aspect of Barcelona's underbelly, and it wasn't until authorities brought them to justice did our empire topple." He paused, thinking of his past, all the while hoping he could get through his current mess with a modicum of good luck. "It seems only fitting I picked up the pieces, didn't it?"

True to Simonetta's investigative methods, he didn't answer.

"So," Borja continued, "it seemed the perfect opportunity when Miranda approached me several years ago to run the poaching operation in Ireland, Canada, and the States."

"What kind of money?"

"You mean what's she worth?"

Javier nodded, knowing his answer didn't really make any difference—it was how much he knew of the organization's inner workings that mattered.

"More than you and I can imagine, Detective. She's as shrewd as the day is long, and not to be trusted . . ." Then?

Sealing the coffin.

"Just ask Silvio Socorro."

Simonetta glanced at Decklin—neither he nor Walsh mentioned the name. "Explain." Of course, he was familiar with the Spanish operative, yet deemed it foolish to confirm.

Borja was quiet for a moment, knowing he opened a can of worms never to be recapped. "Let's just say he did Miranda's bidding—most of the time." It seemed prudent to leave his own name out of it—no sense hanging himself.

"Where is he now?"

A smile. *Does he really not know,* Borja wondered as he assessed the three detectives. But, with the next thought, he knew it couldn't be. "You know quiet well, Detective—Silvio Socorro died at the hands of Miranda Byrne."

Nailing the coffin.

Using the binos he always kept in his truck, Finn Kildare watched as Miranda piled scraggly sticks of driftwood in her arms, then disappear through the cottage door. *It's going to take a lot more than that,* he silently admonished, knowing she would soon be out for more. The problem was, however, he really didn't have time to play a useless waiting game— meaning he had a choice to make. Sell out Miranda's location to Walsh, who would make sure Decklin Kilgarry received the information? Or, make the best use of his time by taking care of business himself? As much as he would've liked to make good on his second option, it was, however, more prudent to keep out of the line of fire until he was needed.

With one last look, he returned to his truck, then drove quietly away, leaving no trace of his presence other than a few tracks in the muddy road. Though he didn't see a vehicle at the cottage, it was common to have a some sort of protection from the weather, usually to the back of the main home. What cued him she drove?

Another set of tire tracks on the same road.

Grateful for the thirty minutes back to his workroom, Kildare immediately brewed a pot of tea, settling in to figure out exactly what he would say to Detective Walsh. Truth was always the best route, but, when in doubt, it seemed the less attractive option, especially in his particular situation. Still, with renewed vigor, he again silently vowed to protect his village no matter his personal cost.

Tapping the screen on his cell, his call immediately patched into voicemail. "Walsh? It's Finn . . ."

Chapter 28

There comes a point in any investigation when the stand-off ceases and one party acquiesces to the other—and, that's the way it was when Carmine Borja decided to posture for immunity. After all, if it weren't for him, Spanish authorities wouldn't have a chance in hell of making charges stick against Miranda Byrne, or anyone else in her organization. No—without Carmine, they had no chance of a conviction. "Before I continue, Detective Simonetta, I feel we have important things to discuss . . ."

Javier smiled, then focused on the visiting detectives. "You hear that, Gentlemen?"

Two nods. "We did."

"Sounds like he's ready for a plea deal—what do you think?"

"But, does he deserve one? I don't think he told us everything he knows," Decklin commented, smiling.

"Agreed." Simonetta again turned his attention to Borja, who was listening intently to the conversation. "So, Carmine—what do you have in mind?"

"Borja grinned, certain of his negotiating position. "You have nothing without me—and, I will accept nothing less than immunity." A cagey maneuver—albeit a faulty one—certain he could craft a believable story to save his ass.

"Immunity? Well—I'm not certain we can go there." Simonetta kept his eyes on Borja, knowing he hit a nerve. "I think there's much more you have to say . . ."

"Like what?"

"Well, for starters, who's involved in your Cobh operation?"

Borja remained silent, mentally cycling through who within their operation would be of interest. "Very few, Detective—Miranda Byrne is a cagey woman."

"Meaning?"

"She's well aware the fewer operatives involved, the less likely she is to fail—and, as you might suspect, failure isn't an option for her."

"How did you get involved?" As tiresome as it may seem, it always proved fruitful to corroborate statements made throughout an interrogation. If they stacked up?

The truth.

Probably.

"It's like I said, Detective, my family was deep into Barcelona's underworld long before Miranda came into my life. And, there's a reason I caught her eye..."

"Why was that?"

"Because I'm a man who gets things done—as my mother used to say, I lack a certain sentiment for other people. The way I see it, they come, they go—and, as long as I get what I need from them, I care little about their lives."

"Charming."

"It's a lifestyle that works for me—without attachment, I am free to conduct business as I see fit."

"Did Miranda get in your way?" Javier didn't take his eyes from Borja, knowing his questions were finally getting to the person many must have hated.

"If she did, chances are good you wouldn't be here speaking with me—like her, I'd be long gone. It's only a matter of luck, Detective, that you found me..."

As much as Simonetti wanted to comment, he refrained, knowing Borja was merely self-aggrandizing. "Tell me about Dominic Delgado."

A laugh. "Delgado?" Carmine paused, thinking of the little worm of a man whom he despised. "The rank he achieved in our organization was exactly where he needed to be."

"What rank was that?"

Another chuckle. "The bottom, Detective."

"So, he wasn't a significant player..."

"Delgado wasn't a significant anything—although, I'm certain he desired to be—and, Miranda knew it. She played him like a pro, bringing him into the fold, paying him just enough to keep him satisfied." Again, a brief pause. "The truth is Dominic Delgado was as malleable as a piece of gum—stretch him one way, and he did what he was told. Stretch him another? You know what I mean . . ."

Javier took a swig of water, then glanced at Decklin and Walsh. "What about Smokey Alvera?"

"Alvera is an idiot—all he's good for is slinging fish guts, and paying attention to what goes on around him. Completely expendable, should the situation arise . . ."

As Decklin and Walsh listened to Carmine Borja divulge particulars, both were struck by his willingness to give Miranda up to authorities. Unfortunately, while there was supposed, useful information, whether any of it could be corroborated was a different game.

"So, about my immunity . . ." Borja triumphantly eyed the detectives, certain he deserved such special treatment.

Of course, Simonetta had no intention of affording Carmine Borja anything except a cell in a place he wouldn't want to be—he didn't need to know that, however. With purposeful intent and just loud enough for Borja to hear, Detective Javier Simonetta tapped his cell, carried on a brief conversation, then tapped the cell screen again, watching it fade to black.

Permission granted.

"You're a lucky man," Detective Simonetta commented, knowing the permission would undoubtedly be rescinded at some point in the future. It was obvious Carmine Borja wasn't the brightest, and he'd undoubtedly screw up with authorities somewhere along the line.

Only a matter of time.

So, for the next hour, Carmine Borja continued to spill his guts, false relief from prosecution loosening his lips. By the time he finished telling what he knew, nothing was left to conjecture, and the three detectives were certain all poaching operations in Cobh—as well as Canada and the States—would soon cease.

"Thank you for your cooperation, Mr. Borja—but, as you probably suspected, your part isn't over." A pause, then a directive. "Please open the door, Detective Walsh . . ."

Seconds later?

Detective Simonetta respectfully escorted Carmine Borja from his villa to an awaiting, official vehicle, advising him of his rights. As Decklin and Walsh watched, Decklin could've sworn he heard Simonetta comment on Borja's new, future digs.

Permanent new digs.

"You're a good man," Decklin said, smiling, as he shook Detective Simonetta's hand. "You changed a lot of lives today—we can't thank you enough." Then, goodbyes—he and Walsh departed, each certain Carmine Borja would live the rest of his days inside prison walls.

"It was easier than I thought," Decklin commented as they pulled away from the precinct. "In the end, it was nothing but arrogance tipping his hand . . ."

Walsh chuckled as he checked his phone for messages. "Hold on, mate—you're never going to believe this!" A pause. "Finn Kildare left a message to call him immediately . . ."

"Well, don't keep the man waiting!" Decklin turned left before the road became a dead end, then pulled into sparse traffic. "You want lunch?

"Aye! Interrogations always make me hungry—even when I'm not the one doin' the interrogating!" Seconds later, he tapped his cell, then connected. "Finn—Graham Walsh." Without informing Kildare, Detective Walsh put the call on speaker. "What can I do for ya?"

For the next thirty minutes, Finn Kildare summarized his involvement in Miranda Byrne's poaching operation, leaving nothing to the imagination as be brought Kilgarry and Walsh up to speed. "Is she still there?" Walsh glanced at Decklin as he asked.

"Aye—and, knowing her, she's not going anywhere for a while."

So much for lunch.

As much as Decklin would've liked to include Connor and Alannah O'Quinn in details of the investigation, it was for their safety he chose not to do so. "Although, the both of you aren't currently in the bullseye of anything," he assured them, "I think it's best if Walsh handles the salient points of his investigation . . ."

"Does that mean you're out of it," his cousin asked. "I hope so!"

"Well, for the most part—there are still a few things to figure out and clean up, but, by the end of the week? I dare say salmon poaching in our little village will be a thing of the past . . ."

"It's sad, though . . ."

Connor glanced at his wife. "What is?"

"Well, although I don't feel much about Dominic Delgado, it's sad Keegan and Wingo had to lose their lives over this whole mess . . ."

"I know—and, for what it's worth, I don't think either one of them really had any idea of what they were getting into . . ."

The three were silent as they remembered the past year, Decklin barely believing he'd been in the village that long. "Walsh has his work cut out for him, that's for sure—but, he's a good man. I know he'll make the arrests happen . . ."

Just as Alannah was about to comment, Decklin's cell vibrated and, quickly, he checked his messages. "I have to go," he apologized, grabbing an apple muffin from the lazy Susan placed in the middle of the kitchen table. "May I?"

Alannah laughed, then shooed him out the door. "Come back in one piece," she ordered, watching him as he walked down the walkway to his car, a funny feeling beginning to rise.

Without turning, he waved, knowing he and Walsh were walking into the proverbial lion's den. "Wish us luck," he muttered.

"Wish us luck . . ."

Aidan McNamara always prided himself for being in the right place at the right time, calling such providential opportunities nothing more than pure luck. And, so it was when he spied Finn Kildare's truck heading north out of the village—suspicion began to mount. But, it wasn't until a few moments later, recognizing Graham Walsh's unmarked vehicle, he decided to follow. The only problem was there were so few cars on the road, it was tricky remaining undetected—yet, somehow, he managed.

Staying well back from Finn's sight line in the rear or side view mirrors, he followed two sets of tire tracks that turned off the main road. Even though there were no vehicles in sight, he slowed, scanning the area, knowing exactly where the muddy road was leading. *The cottage*, he thought, wondering how a ramshackle place like that could spike Walsh's interest. His next thought, however, was one of concern. Suddenly, he knew to stop, no longer willing to take an associated risk. *Something ain't right . . .*

Although the cottage was one hundred or so yards away from his current position, Aidan knew sound would still carry even if muffled by mist. If anyone were paying attention?

Busted.

On foot, he stealthily skirted the road by keeping close to a few sparse trees barely wide enough to conceal his body, keeping his eyes on the road. Within minutes, the cottage came into view—no cars. No trucks. No nothin'...

Except an anemic wisp of smoke spiraling from a stove's chimney.

Then, as if watching action on a film set, Graham Walsh appeared on the left side of the cottage, weapon drawn, Decklin Kilgarry mirroring him on the right. *Smart*, Aidan silently lauded the two detectives. *Approach from the rear so no one can see...*

Quickly, both men approached the only door, one on each side. Then?

All hell.

Even with fog-muffling sound, there was no mistaking Walsh's voice. "Miranda Byrne! This is the police!"

Nothing.

"Miranda Byrne! I repeat! This is the Cobh police!"

Again, nothing. Realizing their only option, Graham glanced at Decklin. "On three?"

Decklin nodded, shifting his weight slightly and, with his fingers, he counted down.

One. Two. Three.

With one, fluid movement, Graham Walsh kicked in the door, weapon still drawn. "Miranda Byrne!"

A second of silence.

Then, a crushing blast from a shotgun, blowing a massive hole in Detective Graham Walsh, opening his stomach wide enough to see the great outdoors.

Instinctively, Decklin entered, pivoted, then fired, not quite believing what was unfolding in front of him. Miranda crumpled, a perfect shot delivered to center mass. There was no question Walsh was dead, but Miranda?

With luck, she'd survive.

At the sound of the shotgun blast, Aidan McNamara and Finn Kildare appeared out of nowhere, both instantly available to help. "This ain't gonna be good," Aidan yelled to Finn as they met at the end of the short lane leading to the cottage.

By the time they reached the decrepit porch, Decklin Kilgarry was on his knees beside his fallen friend, his face ashen with shock. Blood and body tissue spattered cottage walls, Walsh's weapon knocked from his hand across the room.

"Kilgarry!" Finn called to the detective, he and Aidan unsure if it were safe to enter.

Nothing.

"Kilgarry! Walsh!"

Moment's later, Decklin emerged from the cottage, blood staining his clothes, his shoes tracking bloody prints onto the porch. In that moment, Finn and Aidan knew.

"Call the authorities . . ."

Chapter 29

Decklin Kilgarry sat quietly, knowing he had no right to be there, but there was nothing that could keep him away. Even so, no one on the Cobh police force felt like kicking him out, once word began to travel.

He watched Miranda breathe, her chest rising and falling with shallow rhythm. By the grace of God his shot missed vital organs, yet it was catastrophic enough to completely incapacitate her, rendering her helpless at the scene.

Good thing, too.

As with any small town, news of Walsh's murder trickled through the streets, villagers slowly arriving at the precinct to pay their respects. Although few knew what would wind up to be the true consequences of their police detective's death—the end of salmon poaching in Cobh—there was still much to investigate. And, sadly, the truth of it was Decklin had little faith in a force with no leader.

"Kilgarry?" Finn Kildare stood in the intensive care unit's doorway to Miranda's room, his voice a whisper as if honoring someone too soon passed.

Decklin didn't look at him, keeping his eyes on Miranda.

"I know this isn't a good time," Finn continued, "but, when you're ready, we need to talk . . ."

Finally, Decklin acknowledged him. "Thank you . . ." Recalling the scene, Decklin envisioned Finn Kildare and Aidan McNamara taking charge, Kildare keeping watch over Miranda while Aidan attended to Decklin, although he seemed more shaken than hurt.

Not for long, however.

By the time paramedics arrived, Decklin had everything under control, providing police and the coroner with salient details. But, by the time he was checked out at the hospital and back at the O'Quinn's?

The incident was taking its toll.

"I can't believe this!" Alannah's eyes welled as she recalled Graham Walsh sitting at their kitchen table only a few days prior. "This can't be happening!"

Connor scooted his chair closer to hers, placed his arm around her, then focused all of his attention on Decklin. "Tell us what happened . . ."

So, for the next hour, Decklin recounted his time in Barcelona with Walsh and their conversation with Carmine

Borja, as well as their eventual visit to the broken down cottage outside of Cobh. "Miranda Byrne had no intention of turning herself in," he commented. "It's not who she was . . ."

"Oh, I can imagine what kind of person she was," Alannah blurted, her sorrow deepening.

"Of course, we don't really know much about her, but, according to Borja, she was one driven woman . . ."

Alannah shot her cousin a look. "You speak of her with admiration?" It was the first time since Decklin arrived in Cobh a year prior, she spoke harshly to him.

Gently, he took her hand. "No—there's nothing about Miranda Byrne I admire. I simply meant . . ."

"We know what you meant . . ." Connor smiled. "We're glad you're okay."

Diffused.

Two hours later? Decklin Kilgarry sat at Miranda's bedside, praying she would awaken. It turned out injuries from Decklin's gunshot were more invasive than previously realized, resulting in a coma by the time she reached the emergency ward at Cobh Community Hospital.

"You called Walsh," Decklin suddenly commented without looking at him. "What did you want?"

Finn gestured to another chair. "May I?"

A nod.

"Well, I called to warn him—and, you, I suppose, because I knew you took a train out of town. It wasn't hard to figure out you went to Dublin Airport—and, with a mate who works in ticketing?" A pause. "I had your destination in no time . . ."

Finally, Decklin focused his attention away from Miranda, placing it squarely on Kildare. "Okay—but, you wanted to talk to Walsh. About what?"

"The fact Miranda was about to hightail it out of the country—at least, I thought she was. When I called her to let her know you were in Barcelona, there was a coldness I hadn't heard before and her decisions were questionable. But, when she dismissed my concern—or, faux concern, I should say—I knew things were about to take a turn."

"I'm afraid I don't understand—what exactly was your relationship with Miranda?" Then, it clicked. "You were underground?"

"Yes, but not in the way you might imagine."

"Enlighten me . . ."

"Well, it goes back to when poaching began to be a problem in Cobh . . ."

"Five years ago?"

Finn nodded. "Maybe a bit longer—I think Miranda's organization tested the waters, so to speak, long before she inserted herself in a concerted effort to destroy our village."

A prolonged silence.

"I don't know what it was, but, the first time I saw her at the Daft, there was something about her that didn't set right." Another silence. "I'm tellin ya, Decklin—ice clogs that woman's veins, and there was nothin' that could thaw 'em out. Still isn't . . ."

"When did you figure out her M.O.?" By his question, it was clear Detective Decklin Kilgarry was in full-blown cop mode.

"Oh, it took me awhile—at least a year."

"What tipped you off she was running a sophisticated poaching operation?"

"When fishermen's profits declined to the point of changing lives—mine included. I suspected, of course, but I didn't truly understand the scope of it until quite a while after she landed in town." Finn focused on Decklin, then glanced at Miranda. "It's far-reaching . . ."

"So, you . . ."

Suddenly, Miranda twitched, both men keeping a watchful eye. But, that's all it was—an involuntary twitch.

"Let's just say," Finn continued when they realized there was no cause for alarm, "I made her acquaintance. Of course, it was a risky move because I knew all too well someone like Miranda Byrne would never have anything to do with someone like me." He focused at Miranda, keeping his eyes on her as he spoke.

"Go on . . ."

Finn hesitated, as if what he was about to say would make a difference. "I was a bad boy from the docks, Detective—ask anyone around here who's known me since I was a lad. They'll tell you—so, it made perfect sense for me to keep up that persona. The truth is, however, during the time I was gone from my village so many years ago, I became someone my fellow villagers wouldn't recognize. I attended university, learned the ways of the world, then return to help those employed within my village's fishing industry."

"An activist?"

"You can call it that, although I prefer to think of myself a little more logical . . ."

"So—you made a play for Miranda?"

Finn smiled. "A rather crass way of putting—but, yes. We forged a relationship of a certain sort, our reasons for doing so not dissimilar. Yet, if she learned of my true intent, I'd wind up like Keegan and Wingo . . ."

"Then, why?"

Finn was quiet for a moment, then looked Decklin squarely in his eyes. "Because it made sense she would need someone on the inside to make her plan work—someone who knew the industry inside out. A local—I could play her while she played me."

As Finn spoke, what Decklin and Walsh tried so hard to figure out began to crystallize. "You embedded?" A smile. "Pardon the pun . . ."

Kildare chuckled, tension beginning to lift. "So to speak, I suppose—but, that's why I brought Keegan Sullivan into my fold. I needed someone who could work the trawlers, keeping eyes and ears on my target." Finn paused, a smile on his lips. "I'm sure you felt my presence on more than one occasion . . ."

Immediately, Decklin recalled feeling as if someone were watching. "So, it was you—I caught you on camera. You were lucky . . ." Decklin's turn to smile, but only momentarily. The only thing on his mind was getting to the truth. "You mentioned the target—who?"

"Anyone who offered money—plus, I also kept my eyes peeled for deckhands flashing wads of cash in the bars. If there's one thing I know about fisherman, it's their love of drink . . ."

As Finn spoke, Decklin recalled Walsh's conversation with Aidan McNamara months prior. "Aidan suspected."

"Aye—I tried to talk to him about it, but things didn't go according to plan."

"Why did you need to speak with him?"

"Because I needed to find out what he knew about Smokey Alvera..."

"Why?"

"I needed to deflect attention away from me. As things began to heat up, Detective Kilgarry, I found myself in a precarious position. I couldn't trust you, so I needed to proceed on my own—and, I needed to find out exactly what Aidan McNamara knew about his daughter's murder." Finn paused, thinking. "That's why I threw Smokey Alvera under the bus—although, it was clear he had nothing to do with it other than being a messenger."

"Aidan confided to Walsh his daughter sold her soul to the devil..."

"Indeed, she did—Dominic Delgado. I had my eye on him the second he landed in the village—and, early on, when I saw him at the Daft talking to Miranda on more than one occasion, I knew it was more than a client relationship."

Decklin grabbed the bottle of water he kept on the floor by his chair, taking a few gulps. As he listened, he was struck by Finn Kildare's intelligence, as well as his ability to devise a workable plan. "How long after Miranda landed in town did Delgado show up?"

"A couple of months. Which tells me she got what she came for—she determined Cobh was ripe for the pickin'. Knowing that, she inserted a few more people—the most notable being Smokey. When I recognized what was going on, it was up to me to counteract..."

"Tell me about Smokey—he was on our radar."

"As well he should've been, mate—he's a nasty piece of work, although one wouldn't suspect it just to look at him." A pause. "The trouble with Smokey is he's not the brightest bulb . . ."

"Well, he's smart enough to stay on the fringes."

Finn nodded. "That's true—he was also responsible for choosing the trawler most likely to fail, then swooping in to save the day. Miranda told me more than once he was exactly what she needed—and, she paid him well for his efforts. Always dangling carrots, though. That's what kept him around . . ."

Decklin said nothing, knowing damned well Smokey Alvera cut out of Cobh the second word of Walsh's murder hit the streets. Making a mental note of Finn's characterization of the Spanish fisherman, there was a pretty good chance he'd return to Barcelona.

Not the brightest move.

"So," Decklin commented as he tried to place events in chronological order, "if I understand you correctly, you inserted Keegan Sullivan on Wingo McNamara's trawler to see if Smokey would yield information. Is that about it?"

"Exactly. I never intended for Keegan to come to any harm—he and I had been in this village since our youth, and he was one of Cobh's own. Same with Wingo . . ."

As Decklin listened, he realized why Finn Kildare piqued his interest the first time they met at the O'Quinn's.

Kildare was playing a role.

Duplicity.

"But, something interesting happened," Finn continued. "New deckhands began showing up out of nowhere, eager to work on certain trawlers..."

"Wingo's?"

A nod. "Among others. But, it was no secret for the last few years her trawler was in trouble—the McNamaras have been in Cobh forever, and everyone who knew her realized something was wrong."

"Wrong how?"

"Well, losing money and possibly her trawler was weighing on her mind. She, too, began drinking more than normal, running her mouth at the bars." Finn paused. "Oh, she railed against the poachers—yet, when Sean Braniff showed up last year? He was the answer to her prayers, and he introduced her to Dominic Delgado. She needed money in her pocket, and Delgado was the one doling out the cash..."

"I recognize Braniff's name—he was her deckhand?"

Finn nodded. "New last season—that was when the shit really started to hit the fan for Wingo, and she would've done anything to hold onto her trawler. Her business..."

"Apparently, she did."

"Yes—Sean Braniff was Dominic Delgado's plant. Anything he heard, he funneled it back to Delgado. In turn, he made sure Miranda knew exactly what was transpiring on the trawlers."

Again, both men took a moment to glance at Miranda, Decklin finally asking the question that could derail the veracity of Finn's story. "Who killed Keegan Sullivan?"

"Silvio Socorro."

Although Socorro's name surfaced during Carmine Borja's interview, neither considered the idea he was responsible for anyone's death. "What about Wingo?"

"Socorro."

"Delgado?"

"One and the same—by orders of Miranda Byrne, of course."

Decklin said nothing for a few seconds, trying to fit the pieces together. "Tell me about him . . ."

"Socorro? Not much to tell—mainly because I don't know much. Only the quality of his work . . ."

"Did Braniff know about Miranda?"

Finn shook his head. "I doubt it—she was very careful, and gave specific orders that no one should ever know of her involvement. Subsequently, no one did—and, now that I think about it, Sean Braniff appeared on the Cobh fishing scene at the same time I brought Ryan Murphy into my organization for the same reason. I needed someone to keep eyes and ears open, paying particular attention to anyone new on the trawlers. My antennae were already up when it came to Wingo, but I needed to make certain she wasn't the only one targeted."

"Was she?"

"No—but, her situation provided me the best opportunity to take down Miranda Byrne."

"Did Murphy provide what you needed?"

"At times—he turned me onto Wingo's fishing illegally, led to specific waters by none other than Sean Braniff. Who, obviously, was receiving directives from Delgado."

"And, Miranda, no doubt . . ."

"Exactly."

"But, why? Why Keegan and Wingo? Why take either one of them out? Why both?"

Finn sighed deeply, thinking of his old friend. "I suppose I had a bit of responsibility, but considering the circumstances, I had no choice. I had to stop an insidious snake from further invading our waters . . ."

"You were involved with his murder?"

"Yes and no—I had no idea Miranda would send one of her men to do the deed and, in fact, it never occurred to me. I simply thought she wanted to have a conversation with him—you know, to tell Keegan he was doing a good job, then hand him a wad of cash."

"But, that's not what happened, obviously . . ."

"No but, I told her when Keegan and Wingo typically came off the water, and she took it from there."

"Socorro."

A nod.

"Why Wingo? And, for that matter, why Sullivan? He was nothing but a harmless drunk . . ." It occurred to Decklin tradition and allegiance were two things held in high esteem in the small fishing village and, the more he thought about it, the more sense it made for someone unattached to carry out such heinous deeds.

"Simple—both of them had big mouths. Get a little drink in either of them? It was a situation Miranda wouldn't tolerate. You know the power alcohol holds over common sense, Detective—Wingo and Keegan became a threat to

Miranda's organization." A pause. "And, Delgado? I suspect he was quickly becoming a liability . . ."

So, there the two men sat, hoping the woman who made their lives miserable would awaken, making a criminal apprehension possible, even if it weren't immediately. She could, of course, remain in a coma indefinitely, placing Decklin in the position of having to make a decision. Stay in Cobh to see his unofficial case through?

Or, return to life as he knew it.

Chapter 30

Decisions are never easy for anyone, but when they're life-altering?

Much harder.

After funeral services for Graham Walsh, leaving Cobh was something Decklin really didn't want to do, but, as he spent quiet days after the Miranda Byrne ordeal, he knew he must. "You know it's going to take quite a while for a case to be brought against Miranda," he advised Connor and Alannah.

"So, can't you stay until that happens?" Simply talking about Decklin's returning to the States was more than

Alannah could bear.

"No, I don't think that's wise—one of the things I came to realize during my stay here is I can't really run from the source of my discontent. Was it my job? Partially. My marriage dissolving? That's certainly a big part of it—but, as much as I enjoy being here, I understand I'm a cop deep within my soul." He paused, grinning. "Hell, my Cobh ancestors were cops, so it makes sense!"

"Indeed it does!" Connor lifted his orange juice glass. "To new journeys, Decklin Kilgarry! May the wind always be at your back..."

With that, Decklin stood, pulling his cousin into his arms. "You, Alannah O'Quinn, are the shining star of our clan—I'll be back, I promise!"

Well, that did it—Alannah dissolved into tears, her husband getting a bit misty-eyed, as well. "Our door is always open..."

"Do you know Aidan McNamara," Decklin asked his driver.

A huge grin in the rearview mirror. "Who doesn't?"

"Do you know where he lives?"

"Aye—should I take you there?" The driver kept his eyes focused on the rearview, waiting.

"Yes, and please wait—I won't be long."

Within ten, Decklin stood at the McNamaras' door, hoping he could find the right words. No matter his experience as a seasoned cop, speaking with the kin of a murder victim was never easy.

Suddenly, the door opened. "Detective Kilgarry!" Aidan eyed him up and down. "You don't look too much worse for the wear . . ."

Decklin laughed. "Well, it's been a few weeks, so I'm in pretty good shape!" He paused. "May I come in for a minute—I'm on my way to the train station, so I won't stay long."

Aidan stepped aside. "Leaving our village, are ya?"

"Yes—it's time for me to return to the States. But, I wanted to come by and personally offer my condolences—I couldn't before because no one was to know of my involvement with Wingo's murder case. And, Keegan's . . ."

"I appreciate it."

"No one should endure what you have, Aidan, and there's no doubt in my mind Miranda Byrne will spend the rest of her life in prison." He paused, hoping his words didn't sound hollow. "I know it's not much, but, at least, it's some sort of closure . . ."

Aidan offered his hand. "If it weren't for you and Graham, we'd never know. The missus and I appreciate what you did—we can never repay."

"Not needed." As Decklin accepted the handshake, a cool breeze brushed his cheek, touching his heart.

His soul.

"I'll be following the case from afar, but, if there's anything I can ever do for you, Aidan, all you have to do is get in touch—after all, this is my village, too, and I take care of my own."

Tears in his eyes, Aidan McNamara thanked the cop from the States, then watched as he strode down the walk and climbed into his taxi. *No more a stranger*, he thought, watching the cab pull onto the street.

You're no longer from away . . .

Chapter 31

By the time Decklin reached the Dublin Airport, a chilly sleet settled in, wreaking havoc with arrival and departure times. Even so, travelers didn't seem to mind as they claimed their seats at the individual gates. "Excuse me! You dropped this . . ."

Decklin looked up from his book, focusing on a forties something, petite redhead. "I'm sorry . . ."

"Your pen—you dropped your pen." She smiled, holding up an expensive, black pen. "It's a nice one, too!"

Instantly, he laughed, taking the pen from her. "Thank you! I never would've realized it was gone!" Then, he checked his jacket pocket. "Ah! The culprit," he grinned, sticking his index finger through a newly-formed hole in the lining.

Again, he focused on her. "Please, have a seat! I take it you're waiting for a flight?"

She nodded. "Yes—I'm heading back to the States."

"As am I—where?"

"Well, I'm visiting a friend in D.C. for a couple of weeks, then I'll head to the West Coast." She cocked her head. "You seem familiar . . ."

"Really? I don't think we've met before—what's your name?"

"Colbie."

"Last?"

She smiled. "Just Colbie . . ."

NOVELS BY FAITH WOOD

THE COLBIE COLLEEN SUSPENSE MYSTERY SERIES:

The Accidental Audience—Book 1

Chasing Rhinos—Book 2

Apology Accepted—Book 3

Whiskey Snow—Book 4

Chill of Deception—Book 5

At the Intersection of Blood & Money—Book 6

The Scent of Unfinished Business—Book 7

Agenda—Book 8

THE DECKLIN KILGARRY SUSPENSE MYSTERY SERIES

Where Truth Goes to Die—Book 1

LAUNCHING IN SPRING, 2022!!!

SOHO

A Decklin Kilgarry Suspense Mystery—Book 2

PROFESSIONAL ACKNOWLEDGMENTS

CHRYSALIS PUBLISHING AUTHOR SERVICES
Laurie O'Neil, Editor
Cover Design
www.chrysalis-pub.com
chrysalispub@gmail.com

Manufactured by Amazon.ca
Bolton, ON